She was shaking from head to foot

She just wanted to escape. With an inarticulate little sound she sought to pass him, only to feel his hands like steel on her arms and her body crushed mercilessly against his.

"Mark—"

Janet saw his eyes for a moment before his mouth was pressed savagely against her own, dark eyes pitiless in their doubt and ruthlessly demanding in their desire. That one swift, bitter kiss seemed to last a lifetime. She felt it searing through her like a flame, yet turning her heart to ice. Mark was all savage, the bitterness in him obliterating everything else.

She pushed him from her. "Let me go—I think I hate you!"

"Well," he said, freeing her, "that would be a stronger passion than your lukewarm pity."

JEAN S. MacLEOD

is also the author
of the following titles in
HARLEQUIN CLASSIC LIBRARY

The Way in the Dark

JEAN S. MacLEOD

Originally published as Harlequin Romance #541

HARLEQUIN
CLASSIC LIBRARY

TORONTO • LONDON • LOS ANGELES • AMSTERDAM
SYDNEY • HAMBURG • PARIS • STOCKHOLM • ATHENS • TOKYO

Original hardcover edition published by
Mills & Boon Limited 1956
ISBN 0-373-80017-7

Harlequin edition first published September 1960
Golden Harlequin Library edition, Volume XLII,
published September 1973
Harlequin Classic Library edition published April 1980

Second printing May 1981

CHAPTER ONE

IN THE HALF CIRCLE of the bay between the two pine-clad capes the blue water of the Mediterranean glittered in the early-morning sun. There was no sound above the lapping of the tideless sea, no movement, even of a palm frond, in the still air. The silence and the warmth and the scents of exotic flowers added a timelessness to the scene that the girl sitting on the red, sun-baked rock absorbed with an eagerness that suggested she might be storing it in her mind against the bleaker prospect of the future.

She sat with her back to the land and her face turned toward the sea, her slim arms clasped loosely around her knees, her eyes on the lustrous band of the horizon's rim, as if she would penetrate beyond it into a land of her own desiring.

"You look like the mermaid in Copenhagen harbor!"

The man's voice was familiar to her, but she did not turn immediately. Her eyes, still vaguely remote, remained on the shining expanse of sea, but her generous mouth softened in a smile.

"Carved from stone, do you mean?" she asked, turning at last to where he stood on the shingle beneath her.

"Sometimes I wonder." Charles Grantley surveyed her with a humorous smile, although his deeply set gray eyes remained serious. "You've been my aunt's companion for close on six years, Janet, but I wonder if I really know you. If I've ever known you," he added musingly. "You've been the thoughtful nurse to an old lady and my gay companion on infrequent trips along the Corniche d'Or, but sometimes I've imagined that you've never been yourself.''

For a moment she did not answer, looking down at him without seeming to see him, the bright Mediterranean scene blotted from her mind and a cold, bleak moorland taking its place.

"That must be true," she said slowly. "I've never really been Janet Law for the past six years. I've been what my work and my own desire have made me."

"I've no regrets on that score!" Charles hoisted himself onto the red rock beside her, his back to the sun's warmth, his darkly tanned body a complete foil to the smooth honey color of her flawless skin. "You are what I need, Janet. The 'shining rainbow' to the 'restless cataract' of my living. There's no recklessness in you. You are secure and confident in your desires."

She shook her head.

"I used to think so," she said in the low, tranquil voice he admired so much, "but now I know that I am neither confident nor secure, Charles."

"Because of my aunt's death?" he queried, his quick smile an instant dismissal of her problem. "That needn't make the slightest difference, Jan. I've been trying to tell you that since the funeral, but perhaps it is going to take longer than a week for you to believe me. I love you," he went on urgently. "I want you to marry me, Jan. Tomorrow, if you like. We will drive along to Cannes or Nice and arrange it. A ceremony at the Hôtel de Ville and a church service afterward in England, if that is what you wish."

He was offering her the sort of life she had led for the past six years, the sunshine and luxury of this exotic little resort with its feet steeped in the warmth of the blue Mediterranean and its backdrop of pine-fringed hills where olives and vines garlanded the terraces as far as the eye could see. He was offering her security and the things she had coveted all those years ago when her horizon had been bounded by the bleak North Sea and her familiar landscape had been the wild crags and distant fells of the lonely Yorkshire moors.

Charles Grantley was holding out the prospect of further escape, and she knew that she was not going to take it.

Looking up into his thin, handsome face with its decisive chin and humorous, smiling eyes, she found it difficult to refuse him, but her mind had been made up days ago, even before his aunt's death.

"I'm sorry, Charles," she said, her voice nervous and shaken by the force of her sudden emotion. "I thought that we were nothing more than good friends all these years."

He swung around, pulling her into the circle of his arms until his skin burned against her own.

"How could you think that?" he demanded. "You couldn't have been completely blind, Janet. Even when I was away from you, you must have realized that there was only one place I wanted to be." He held her compellingly, as if the very force of his demand might soften her and shake her resolve. "What else can you do?" he asked. "What other sort of life could you possibly want?"

She drew away from him, although he would not release her completely.

"Please let me try to explain," she begged. "It's difficult, Charles, but I've been over it so often in my mind that I'm completely convinced now. I thought that I belonged here, that this was my particular way of life, and while your aunt was alive and I was necessary to her, I knew that I had to stay. But now I have to go."

"When you are necessary to me?" He asked the question, but his compressed lips and slightly narrowed eyes suggested a mounting tension that he found difficult to subdue. "How foolishly women can reason, when you come to think of it!" he exclaimed. "You were content here, Jan. You were happy. So long as my aunt needed you, you were content to remain. What difference has her death really made? Our marriage was inevitable from the start."

"Inevitable?" She repeated the word slowly, as if it had some deep, hidden meaning for her of which he could know nothing. "Is all love—inevitable?"

"More or less." His arms tightened around her, although he was not yet sure that he had won a victory. "You meet, you are attracted, you love. It goes like that, Jan, whether you like it or not!"

"Yes," she said. "Yes, it goes like that," but she was not thinking of Charles Grantley or the blue sky above the Esterels or the scarcely stirring palms. "We can't escape it, can we—ever?"

His hands tightened on her arms.

"Are you trying to tell me that you have been in love before?" he demanded. "That you are still in love?"

She looked away from the searching scrutiny of his eyes, aware that she had seen deepest hurt in their gray depths.

"Before I came to work for your aunt," she said, as if compelled to start at the beginning of her story so that she might command his better understanding, "I lived in Yorkshire, on a farm on the moors, a remote place in the North Riding that was often cut off in winter and was always isolated. It was my home. It was the home given to me by Matthew Langdon and his wife, Harriet. They adopted me when I was a year old, and I lived at Wildfell till I was nineteen."

Her voice wavered and Charles said peremptorily, "I know all this, Janet. You have told me about your adoption by these people before. I know how grateful you felt to them, but you have told me, too, that you felt you had to get away in the end. It was a life of hard work and sometimes privation, wasn't it? Or so I gathered."

A slow color rose in Janet's cheeks, and as if it pained her, she put her hand up and pressed it against the warm, sun-kissed flesh.

"I've suffered agonies of remorse for my ingratitude," she confessed. "Matthew Langdon was a harsh guardian, but he was strictly fair. He believed in work, and the life at Wildfell was not nearly so bleak as I imagined at nineteen. I know now that I wanted to try my wings, and so I flew away, but I have come to regret it since. Harriet Langdon didn't deserve that particular brand of ingratitude for all she had done for me, and indirectly I was the cause of much sorrow to her."

"Because her own family left Wildfell, too?" he queried. "You could not have been the cause of that. Or were you, Jan?" he demanded ruthlessly when she did not answer immediately. "Wasn't there a son who went away? You've told me about him. Was he in love with you, too?"

Her clear blue eyes were suddenly full of tears.

"It was so long ago," she said. "So very long ago."

"Six years. And in that time he has never written to you?"

"No."

"Do you want my advice? Selfish advice, but sane enough for all that. Forget him."

She tried to smile with her lips trembling.

"I've tried. But somehow it isn't any use."

Impatiently he jumped from the rock, his dark brows drawn in a quick frown.

"You're storing up a lot of heartache for yourself, Jan," he warned. "Six years is a long time in a man's life. You were nineteen and he was, presumably, not much older. If you could try to see it as a boy-and-girl affair that just died naturally, it wouldn't hurt so much."

Janet stood tensed and still above him, all the color gone from her face. It was as if he had struck her a vicious physical blow, and her voice was bleak when she answered him.

"If it is dead, then it was I who killed it."

"But you mean to go back and find out?"

"Not only for that reason." Her voice was steadier now, and full of resolve. "I owe it to the Langdons to go back, Charles. I owe it to Harriet Langdon, who brought me up when I was alone in the world, and I owe it to Matthew. He's never shown any sign of forgiving me for my 'base ingratitude' in leaving Wildfell, and perhaps he never will, but he is an old man now, and I feel that I must try to win that forgiveness somehow. They are both getting old. Harriet Langdon was forty when Ruth was born. She thought she was never going to have a daughter of her own and that may have been her reason for adopting me, but Ruth was born a year after I went to Wildfell, and we were always like sisters."

"And the son?" Charles queried, looking out to sea. "Is he still at the farm?"

"I don't know. Mark left Wildfell not long after I went to London, but—he made no effort to find me. I think he quarreled with his father over some stubborn decision of the old man's, but I never really knew. Ruth had left Wildfell by that time, too, driven away by her father's harshness, I think. It must have broken Mrs. Langdon's heart to lose us all so swiftly, and especially Mark."

"Mark Langdon!" Charles mused, looking up at her. "So I've got to bear that name across my heart, Jan, till you've found out how wrong you are!"

"Charles," she said softly, "don't wait. Find someone else who will make you happy, and forget me."

He laughed sharply.

"You have a short memory, Jan! Five minutes ago I gave you the same advice and you would not take it. I haven't much chance of forgetting you," he added, "when you are—just you!" He looked up at her again and smiled. "All the same, I still think you are making a mistake in going to England on this wild-goose chase after an old love. Nobody has ever been successful in turning back the years, Jan, and you've been softened by the life you have led here. These people will seem like strangers to you."

"They couldn't, Charles!" she protested instantly. "They were too much a part of my life before I decided to fend for myself. I've written to Mrs. Langdon every now and then, although I've only had infrequent letters from her. No, they could never seem like strangers," she decided, reassuring herself. "The life at Wildfell was too homely for that."

"Until you disrupted it?" He shot the question at her with all the abruptness of a challenge. "Are you quite sure that they are going to want you back?"

Watching her expressive face change at the cruelty of his probing, he felt remorse, but he still believed her mistaken in this thing she wanted to do. If she had left some bleak Yorkshire dale on a girlish impulse, she had surely found compensation enough in the sort of work she had been doing for the past six years and the life she led as a rich woman's companion. His aunt had loved youth. She had been a generous woman and a patient sufferer, and Janet and she had been friends. What more could Janet want?

He stretched up, putting his hands around her slim waist to help her down from the rock, but he did not take her into his arms a second time. Instead, he picked up her gaily patterned beach robe from the stones at his feet and put it around her shoulders.

The small, protective gesture touched Janet as nothing else could have done.

"Charles," she said, "I'm sorry. I wouldn't have hurt you like this for the world, but—but it's something I *have* to do—a sort of urge I have to obey. All these past few months when I haven't heard from Wildfell I've been wondering if anything has gone wrong there, if Harriet Langdon needs me. It's been gnawing at the back of my mind for weeks, so that I had to write, although I couldn't have gone while your aunt was alive."

"No," he agreed despondently, "you have a deep sense of duty, Janet. It must have been mislaid for a moment when you first left Wildfell."

The faint cynicism in his tone was justified, Janet supposed. She had hurt Charles unwittingly, and perhaps she couldn't really expect him to understand about Wildfell. He had offered her so much by asking her to be his wife.

Closing her eyes, she tried to shut out the lush vision of all that Charles Grantley had to give and the man himself, tall and undeniably handsome, with his dark hair brushed back from a high, intelligent brow and his penetrating gray gaze and smiling, generous mouth. If it was compressed a little now it was because he was disappointed, but there was nothing in his face to compare with the savage anger she had seen in Mark Langdon's six years ago when she had told him that love was not enough to keep her in lonely Comerdale a moment longer.

How little she had known of love then! Her heart twisted at the memory, at the thought of all those days afterward when Mark's name had been written in letters of fire across her heart and she had known that she could not appeal to him for forgiveness, ever.

"Have you had any reply from these people?" Charles asked when they had almost reached the terrace. "Have they invited you back?"

She shook her head.

"It was a difficult letter to write, Charles," she confessed. "I suppose I was asking to go back on the old terms, really, but there was nothing to suggest that I was wanted. Just this sort of—urge within myself that I had to go, that I might be needed."

He glanced up at the pink and white stucco villa above them, sitting there on its graveled terrace above the sea with its green shutters open to admit the morning sunshine and the scent of a thousand flowers.

"I suppose it's mean of me to hope that you are not needed," he said. "Not in England. I won't close the villa, Jan," he added purposefully, "because I believe that you will come back. I still think that you are making a mistake. From what you have told me about Wildfell, I believe you have grown away from it in the past six years, and that would apply to the Langdons, too. Go, by all means, for the holiday you so richly deserve, but come back, my dear, to Cap St. Jean, and I will be waiting."

Janet's eyes were misty as she turned to him.

"I couldn't make such a promise, Charles," she said huskily. "I might not be able to keep it."

"I think you will," he said. "Even if you were once in love with someone else. Six years is a long time in any man's life, and the Mark Langdon who was twenty and in love could conceivably have changed out of all recognition by now."

Janet did not answer. Waiting for the reply to the most difficult letter she had ever written in her life, she felt unsure and restless, yet she was haunted by the conviction that she must return to Wildfell, that she owed this to the Langdons, quite apart from the burning certainty in her heart that Mark Langdon held her life's happiness or misery firmly between his two strong, work-roughened hands.

Two days later a cable arrived at the villa. It was addressed to Janet and her hands were unsteady as she opened it. It said, "Yes, come, if that is what you want," and it was signed simply "M. Langdon."

Old Matthew Langdon had forgiven her, in part, for her former desertion. Janet felt that it was the old man's typically brusque way of accepting her into the family again, although it did not give her any indication of change at Wildfell.

She realized that she did not want it to be greatly changed. She wanted Wildfell as it had remained in her memory all these years, softened a little, perhaps, but not changed.

Nervously yet excitedly she prepared to make the journey to Yorkshire.

"You'll fly, of course," Charles said when he heard her decision. "At least as far as London, and I'll come with you. There are a few things to be cleared up in connection with my aunt's will. The lawyers will want your signature about that small legacy she left you, by the way." He smiled ruefully. "You'll have to see me again, Janet, whether you like it or not!"

She thrust a hand through his arm, squeezing it tightly.

"You've been so kind, Charles," she acknowledged. "I shall never be able to repay you."

"You can try," he suggested, "when you've come to your senses over Mark Langdon."

She found it easier to meet this lighter mood, although she was still profoundly aware of the deeper current that ran beneath it. For the next two days Charles did his best to sustain it. He whirled her around their favorite haunts when her packing was done; to St. Tropez, and inland to Valescure among the vineyards, where the silver Argens flowed parallel to the sea and the gleam of white-sanded beaches flashed through the boles of the pines. He drove her for miles along the seaboard where white luxury cruisers rode at anchor in little harbors, their still reflections duplicated in the azure of deeply sheltered bays. They went beneath tall oleanders to Boulouris, with the grasshoppers chattering like starlings all along the way, and they stood by the little lagoon at Agay and remembered picnics there in the sun with the gentle old lady who would not pass that way again. They swam from the rocks at Le Trayas and walked along the cherry-bordered road to La Napoule, and always the sun shone out of a cloudless sky and Janet was reminded that this had been her life for six impressive years.

Perhaps Charles was trying to point out the fact to her by renewing these memories, but she could not change her mind now. She did not want to change it. The cable that bade her return to England lay in her handbag, underlining the urgency with which she had first thought of returning, and although it did not hold warmth or even welcome, she was determined to go.

She supervised the closing of the villa, barring the green shutters for the last time with a deeply felt sense of loss. She had experienced happiness within these gleaming, sun-warmed walls, and a companionship and sense of well-being that she might never possess again.

Charles came from his hotel in a rented car to pay off the servants, and they drove to Nice in a silence that held much regret. So many little things tugged at the heart-strings when you came to say goodbye, Janet thought, and Miss Emily had been very dear to her.

She thought of the old lady as they boarded the plane, how she would never fly because it was more leisurely to go by boat and train and there was so much time to do these things. She had lived what some might have called an idle life, but perhaps only Janet knew the extent of her personal charities. Charles had visited her often. His work with an international banking firm took him to Paris and Berlin and Rome, which was "on her very doorstep," she had pointed out when they finally settled at Cap St. Jean.

Charles would come here again, Janet mused as the plane gained height over the Alps and the deep blue Mediterranean fell away behind them, but she doubted if she would ever revisit all these loved and lovely spots.

With a swift, almost painful quickening of the heart, she tried to look ahead, but she could not penetrate the future, even in imagination.

Not until she had left Charles in London, however, did she fully realize how completely she had cut herself off from the past six years of her life. "Nobody can hope to go back," Charles had said when they had been discussing Wildfell. Was that true? Was what she had done foolish in the extreme, and would she regret it as soon as she had reached her destination?

I mustn't, she thought. *I mustn't! There can't be any regrets. It was what I had to do.*

As the train thundered northward she tried not to think of Mark Langdon. She had no knowledge of him. Apart from the brief intimation that he had left Wildfell shortly after Janet's own departure for London, Harriet had scarcely ever mentioned her son. In some ways these letters had been difficult to write and receive, Janet reflected. There was a stern side to Harriet, too, which prevented her from discussing Mark because she knew that he had been in love with Janet all those years ago. Her love for her adopted daughter had embraced a deep and generous understanding that had regretted her husband's harshness and had kept them in touch from time to time, but it had not kept her from resenting the hurt to her son. Once, and once only, Harriet had written to say that Mark had returned to the farm, but whether it had been for a holiday or for good Janet had never known. Mark's activities had remained a closed book between them, but it was unlikely that he could have lived in peace with his father.

"Come, if that is what you want," Matthew Langdon had cabled, and, as she journeyed nearer to Wildfell, Janet felt it was an odd command. "If that is what you want." Was it what *they* wanted? There was no softness about Matthew Langdon. He and Mark were as hard as the gray rock on the fells above their moorland home, as bitterly relentless when a wrong had been done.

"Come, if that is what you want."

Once more she drew out the crumpled cable, her eyes lingering on the brief signature at its foot. *I've come on an impulse,* she thought, *but do they really want me after all this time?*

When she reached York the sun was shining and the twin towers of the minster stood out white against a cloudless sky. She had an hour to wait for her connection, and she went out of the station to walk through the arched bar into the walled city she knew so well from many visits in the past. York had been the edge of the world to her in those days, the lovely, ancient gateway to romance. Harriet Langdon had taken her little family there once a year to buy clothes for them and they had made a day of it. A red-letter day. It had remained that way in Janet's mind all these years so that she discarded the thought of food to walk along Lendal and through St. Helen's Square to the marketplace on Pavement Street.

The group of covered wooden stalls was still there, with their fruit and merchandise spread out for all to see and bargain for, and a rush of warmth flooded across her heart as she strolled leisurely between them. Here was the past. It was still the same. Nothing had changed.

She caught the train for Pickering in higher spirits, sitting forward in her seat as familiar landmarks slid past the carriage window. *You can go back, you can go back,* the noisy, turning wheels seemed to say.

There had been no question of her being met at the station. Life on a moorland farm was too busy for that— the life at Wildfell.

Her pulse quickened as memory lured her into the past and the scene changed before her eyes. With the sun full upon them, there was no bleakness about the moors on this golden late-summer day, and the grass had never looked so green. She compared it with the scorched fields of the Esterels and the gray of the sun-bleached scrub along the Corniche d'Or, letting down the carriage window to feel the salt-laden wind from the North Sea blowing in her face. It came straight from the sea, untrammeled by heat or dust, fiercely invigorating, lending its strength to the men who worked in the teeth of it, day after day, winter and summer, year in year out.

Mark, she thought. *Mark*! Her heart lifted with a fierce belonging, claiming that strength as her own.

When she joined the little local bus that would take her to Comerdale, she half expected to see faces she knew, but there were only a few passengers, most of them late holidaymakers riding the last lap after a day's walking across the moor. They would be going on to Goathland, she supposed, to one of the hotels there.

Her own destination was perhaps the remotest point on the whole wide expanse of moorland, and she saw the bus driver glance at her curiously as she got down at the Fox and Hare.

The isolated little inn stood high above the dale on a windswept ridge of moor with not a tree in sight and only a blaze of heather to break the universal green stretching for miles in a rolling plain toward the gray North Sea. Here and there isolated peaks rose along the horizon, the craggy fells of the north that bore no resemblance to any other hills she had ever seen.

Comerdale lay at their feet, hemmed in by them on every side, so that the sun was lost down there at this hour of the day and only the dark shadow of the fells lay across it, making it look even more remote than Janet remembered.

She had expected to be met at the inn. It was seven miles to Wildfell from that point along a narrow, winding road, difficult at the best of times, but burdensome with a bag to carry.

Her eyes left the distant shoulders of the hills and scanned the road, but it lay before her white and deserted, a twisting ribbon dipping and winding through the dale, now lost, now appearing to breast a hill until the pines above Scarton swallowed it up completely.

The road beyond Scarton Grange could not be seen from the Fox and Hare, and so Wildfell, too, was hidden up there on the far side of the dale where the wind swept in from the north and even the hardier pines refused to grow.

Undecided what to do, she waited, listening to the

sound of the bus dying away in the distance. The silence of the moors descended on her like a pall, with only the intermittent bleating of sheep coming from the far side of the dale to break it. The plaintive cry of a curlew circling high above her awakened a host of memories, and a new and powerful emotion choked against her throat, filling her heart with tears. *I wanted to come back, she thought, but perhaps it isn't my country, after all.* She felt a stranger, yet deep down she knew that she belonged.

Born and bred there, how could she feel otherwise? She drew in deep breaths of the moorland air and knew that she had waited for this for a long time.

Turning her back on the silent dale, she looked to the west, where the sun slanted across the heather, turning it to purple fire, and the mellow light gave her renewed courage. When she looked down into the dale again a car was coming toward her along the road from Scarton.

Even from that distance she could see that it was an old, battered vehicle that had made the journey many times, and she strained her eyes, hoping to recognize the driver. Mark?

Her heart raced, only to be stilled to bitter disappointment at sight of the grizzled head that thrust itself from the open window as the driver crashed his gear into second to negotiate the brow of the hill. He pulled up at the inn door, wiping the back of a gnarled hand across an obviously dry mouth.

"Heber!" Janet cried, recognizing him. "You've come from Wildfell to meet me?"

The old man got down from the car. Heber Crookshank had been at Wildfell as long as Janet could remember. "Man and boy," he would have said, "for all of fifty years." He was part of the farm and part of the dale, brown and rugged and hard, like the fell land itself, and the deep emotion that she had known a moment or two ago when she had first looked down into the dale flooded through Janet's heart again.

"I thought someone would come," she said warmly. "I thought it might have been Mr. Langdon, Heber, but you will do just as well!"

He gave her a long, searching look, his eyes screwed up against the sun.

"We got your telegram less nor an hour gone. Jed Barton came frae Thorpe wi' it, ower t'hill. Young maister expected ye, though. He said ye wud come. There be only young Mark noo at Wildfell. T'auld maister be dëad these three months gone, an' t'mistress ta'en to her bed wi' shock, like." He paused, considering the state of affairs at the farm and the changes she had seen in the dale since she had left it six years ago. "Ay," he remarked philosophically, "death has a way o' creepin' up on everybody."

Janet drew in a deep, quivering breath. So Mark was master at Wildfell now, and it had been Mark's cable that had bade her come home!

She could not answer Heber. She could not say that she was sorry that Matthew Langdon was dead, nor ask about Ruth. She felt stunned, rooted to the spot, sorry that she had come, sorry that she had obeyed Mark's brusque summons, which had sounded so like his father that she had never thought to doubt its origin.

In the next instant, however, she knew that she could not be sorry, because she had come in response to a summons that had nothing to do with Mark Langdon's desire. Harriet Langdon needed her.

While she waited for Heber to collect some parcels at the inn, she wondered about Ruth, Harriet's own daughter, whom she had mentioned as seldom as she had mentioned Mark.

"Heber," she asked when the old man reappeared, his lips suitably moistened and a brighter sparkle in his eyes, "is Miss Ruth at Wildfell now?"

Heber made a clucking sound in his throat, which she remembered as his way of expressing impatience.

"Have ye no' hëard? Ye've been ower lang away, I'm thinkin', miss. She's gone t' Canada lang ago, wi'out as much as a goodbye. T'auld maister was flaysome hard on Miss Ruth, but there was no call for her to tak' hersen t'other side o't'world to get shot on him."

Janet remained silent. She could not discuss the Langdons with Heber, however much she wanted to know, and nothing seemed very real but the fact that Mark was in control at Wildfell and had not forbidden her to return.

Her heart thumped and clamored for the truth as the car bumped down into the dale, past the scatter of stone-built houses that was Grimthorpe village and over the ford where the creek lay brown and dark between the gray steppingstones and the few trees the dale could boast. Past Grimthorpe and up the hill toward Scarton.

The Grange gates stood open and the wide pastureland beyond caught a sudden gleam of sunlight pouring in unexpectedly from the west. The slanting golden rays seemed a symbol of the richness that was the Grange land, lying wide and fertile on this more sheltered side of the narrow dale, and Janet found herself contrasting it with the starkness of Wildfell, comparing the two farms as they had been six years ago. In those days, Scarton Grange had seemed to exist in another world, a world of riches and plenty, of which Wildfell knew nothing.

"Are the Ransomes still at the Grange, Heber?" she asked as they skirted the edge of the pine wood. "Or have there been changes there, too?"

She remembered Tom Ransome and his youthful affection for Ruth Langdon, wondering why Ruth should have chosen to put three thousand miles of ocean between herself and someone she had patently adored.

Heber answered her without looking at her this time. His eyes were on the twisting, narrowing road to Wildfell.

"Auld Ransome be dëad, an all. An' young Tom away to London like t'rest o' ye! T'maister has his land noo."

"Mark?"

The word was like an indrawn breath caught swiftly in Janet's throat. So Mark was now rich and prosperous! Her heart sank a little.

When they reached Wildfell it was still the same. The farmhouse itself was built into an open-sided square with the outbuildings huddled about it for protection. It looked remote and bleak standing up there on the ridge of the moor, conceding nothing to comfort, and when the car drew up in the roughly cobbled yard there was no sign of welcome.

Janet wanted to ask about Mark and could not. She left it to Heber to tell her what he would about his new master and to announce her arrival.

Strange, she mused, not to be running through that open doorway to be embraced by Harriet Langdon or frowned upon by Matthew! She could not believe that she was the same person who had drawn water from the spout to carry it, laughing, into the kitchen for a bath. She could not believe that she had run across these moors as a girl with Mark or Ruth at her heels, her hair flying, her cheeks aflame under the rough caress of the wind, and her heart twisted painfully as she remembered the day when Mark, catching up with her, had kissed her on the lips for the first time.

They had stood staring at each other afterward, breathless and overwhelmed by the intensity of sudden desire, and then she had laughed nervously and run away. Mark, surprised, had come after her, but she had been too quick for him. She had stood, with burning cheeks and pounding heart, in the big barn till his long shadow had passed the door, and then she had wondered what he would have done if he had caught her. Would he have kissed her again?

Thinking about Mark was like coming up against a stone wall. She did not know what she would find on the other side—the other side of six eventful years.

"Best to go in," Heber told her. "Mrs. Langdon be in sitting room at this time o' day."

Janet stepped over the threshold directly into the "houseplace," which had always been the heart of the farm, her pulses quickening as she saw that nothing had changed. Evidence of the same almost primitive way of life that Wildfell had known under Matthew Langdon was still there in the home of his son. It was a man's house.

She stood in the deserted kitchen, looking around her for a full minute, aware that there was no sign of a meal having been prepared for her coming nor, indeed, much of a fire in the wide grate with which to cook one. The rafters above her head were hung with cured hams, as they always had been, but there was a deserted air about everything that disconcerted her till she heard a voice she knew.

"Is that anyone for me?"

She ran into the adjoining sitting room, flinging her arms about the thin, frail figure on the couch beneath one of the windows, her breath caught up in sudden tears. Harriet Langdon waited, stroking her hair with a patient hand.

"And so you've come, Janet?" she said quietly, at last. "I felt you would."

"I've wanted to." Janet's voice sounded thick and muffled, but she lifted shining eyes to the tired gray ones watching her so eagerly. "I've wanted to come for more than a year, but I couldn't have left Miss Pope when she needed me most. We both realized that it wouldn't be for long, and she depended on me so much at the end."

"Yes, Janet," Harriet said. "You did the right thing. You could not have left the old lady to die alone when she had been so good to you."

Janet knelt down beside the couch. Harriet's frailness had shocked her when she had first come into the room, but now she saw it as something that had been arrested by the healing power of joy. All the same, she had a confession to make.

"I should never have gone away, Mother Harriet." The old name slipped out naturally, as if she had used it no further back than yesterday. It was the name Harriet Langdon had taught her to use as a child, explaining it when she came to explain the fact of her adoption in later years so that Janet could reject either name if it pleased her. It had remained Mother Harriet because neither had thought to change it. "I can't understand my ingratitude. I cannot understand how I could have thought that there was anything like Wildfell in all the world."

Harriet smiled. She had a plain face with sparse gray hair drawn away from it into a severe knot at the back of her head, but any severity of expression was immediately redeemed by her eyes. Wise, kindly eyes they were, that had seen far too much of the world's sorrow to condemn a youthful mistake.

"It hurt Mark," she said, but that was all. No question of her own hurt. No reproaches.

It was several minutes before Janet realized that there was tension between them after that first all-forgiving greeting. Harriet had welcomed her eagerly enough, but there was still a suggestion of reserve, a hint of something withheld which cut like a knife across Janet's sensitive heart.

In the short, painful silence that fell between them, a child's laughter echoed from the field beyond the window.

Janet got up and crossed the room, her breath held as she looked out over the paddock where Mark Langdon had taught her to ride as a girl. She saw the familiar stretch of rough grass, and at the end of it a child on a small pony, a boy of about four, with the high Langdon brow and Mark's fiery hair and a look of Mark about him that was unmistakable.

Her breath caught in her throat and an anguished question trembled on her lips.

"Mark's boy," Harriet said quietly. "He's been teaching him to ride."

It seemed to Janet that all the light had faded from the dale and a cold wind blew down across the hills. So Mark had married? Her heart twisted with the bitter intensity of her love for this man who had once been her devoted slave, and it was minutes before she could ask the obvious question.

"And his wife?" she said.

Harriet Langdon looked away from her agonized gaze.

"We never knew her," she answered. "We still don't know what happened to Mark when he left the dale. The three years he spent in London are a closed book. He will not speak of them, but he came back changed out of all recognition. He lives only for the boy now. There's no doubt that he bought the Grange so that the child might have it one day."

Janet could not speak. She felt that her entire world

was crumbling before her eyes, yet there was no reason why she should have demanded Mark's fidelity. *Only that I loved you, Mark*, she cried mutely. *I loved you and I went away!*

"I can't get up onto my feet," Harriet said, "but you know your way around. Nothing has changed."

Only my life. Only the future, Janet thought as she turned away. *I came back because you needed me, but I came, too, because of Mark. Because I loved him and I couldn't live without him!*

Slowly she made her way up the wide staircase, seeing how threadbare the old carpet had become and how much the fine old woodwork needed polishing. Who looked after Mark and the child? Who was there to take care of Harriet now that she was almost bedridden?

She supposed that she would find the answer to all these things when she came down again, but would she ever find the answer to the riddle of Mark Langdon?

Or wasn't it easy? Wasn't it just that he had ceased to love her while she had gone on loving? She had tossed his love back in his face six years ago, and he had accepted it, offering it, in time, to someone else.

What had this other love of Mark's been like, and where was she now that Mark was at Wildfell alone? The fierceness of her own momentary jealousy appalled her, and when she had reached her old, familiar room she stood with her back against the door, burying her face in her hands as if to shut out thought.

When she looked up again, struggling for composure, she saw that the bed had been crudely made up by an unpracticed hand and there was a fire in the narrow grate. Her eyes stung with tears. Was this Mark's only welcome?

Lifting her suitcase, she put it on a chair under the dormer window, automatically standing on tiptoe to look out. The yard beneath her was deserted, but before she could draw back a man's deep voice sounded from the direction of the paddock. He was talking to the child, and Janet's hand flew to her throat as she looked down at them. The tall, spare man in immaculate riding breeches was surely Mark, yet six years had wrought such a change in him that she almost doubted the evidence of her own eyes.

Here was no hesitant, shy daleland youth such as she had known and laughed with in former days, but a man of authority, accustomed to command, with an air about him that suggested a certain ruthlessness that made her pounding heart stand still. The word "mature" darted into her mind, but this was more than maturity. It was a studied determination in the man to bend life to his will. The Mark she had lost was not this stranger with the grim mouth and almost forbidding exterior, and already she was afraid of meeting him.

Hesitating at the top of the wide staircase before she went down, she watched him come into the hall with the child on his shoulder, and for an instant the old Mark was there. His head flung back, he met the challenge of the child's laughter with an answering smile on his lips that changed him completely, and then he looked up to where she stood. The smile faded, and his thin, dark face was almost saturnine as their eyes met and held and she saw a man who had indeed changed.

Silhouetted against the open window, he might have been Matthew Langdon come to life again, so stern and harsh had Matthew's son become in those intervening years.

Without speaking, he waited for her to descend the stairs, his indifferent gaze never wavering as he set the child down on the rug between them.

"Mark," Janet said uncertainly, unable to bear his silent scrutiny any longer, "it's nice to see you again."

How banal the conventional greeting seemed, met by those eyes and his continuing silence! But what else could she have said? In other circumstances she could have cried, "Mark, you sent for me! You wanted me to come back." But she knew that he did not want her, and if he needed her at Wildfell it was not for himself.

"Jonathan," he said, laying a hand on the child's ruffled hair, "this lady has come to look after us. It is extremely kind of her, and you will appreciate the fact all the more when you consider that she left Yorkshire six years ago because she could not bear the life at Wildfell. It was rough and primitive, and she preferred a softer way of living."

The child looked at him questioningly for a moment before small dancing lights broke in the clear blue eyes and he laughed.

"That isn't true," he said distinctly. "Wildfell's grand!"

"It depends how you look at life, Jonathan," Mark said as the boy ran off through the doorway into the garden.

Janet stood very still, facing this almost suave stranger who bore no resemblance to the man she loved. Mark had hardened; he had adopted the polished manners of a gentleman, but beneath the surface there was something savage in his contempt of her. He had not forgiven her, as she had so fondly hoped, and he had never been able to stoop to pretense. Why, then, had he agreed to her return?

"I've seen your mother," she told him unevenly. "I'm sorry about her illness, Mark. How long has she been like this?"

"Since my father died." His cold scrutiny was now complete, but he did not move toward the living room. It seemed that he had something more to say to her before they joined Harriet Langdon for their evening meal. "She is incapable of doing a great deal for herself, but apart from that she needs companionship. She brought up two daughters," he continued harshly, "and at least one of them owes it to her to be here."

"I'll do my best, Mark." Janet had to fight back sudden tears, but she would not let him see how much he had hurt her. "I would have come back long ago, but my employer was ill. She depended on me, and I felt that I had to stay with her, especially toward the end."

She felt that her explanation had hardly reached him. He was not at all concerned with what she had done during the past six years, and something forlorn and hopeless died in her as she looked at him.

"You'll find everything here very much as it has always been," he told her abruptly. "Wildfell has not changed. It has been our home for so long that we would not wish it to change. Martha Crosby has been coming from Kirby Allerton to do the rough work once a week, but she has been laid up with arthritis for the past month and Heber has been doing what he could. There is no one else."

"You mean that—you've been cooking your own food?"

He regarded her amusedly.

"Heber and I between us," he agreed. "Men are not the helpless creatures you apparently imagine, Janet. Nor are they wholly dependent on a woman."

She bit her lip.

"But the two farms? Surely you had enough work to do outside?"

"More than enough. But there are twenty-four hours in a day. Besides, I have a farm manager at the Grange."

"You have done well, Mark, buying the Grange in so short a time to add to Wildfell."

Something changed in his face. She would have said that it grew sterner if that had been possible, but perhaps the expression only sharpened.

"The two farms make a tidy bit of land," he agreed. "Something to pass on."

"To Jonathan?" She thought of the child with a sudden wistfulness. "He's a Langdon, Mark."

The gray-green eyes met her instantly, the thick red brows drawn above them in a swift frown.

"That is what I hoped for," he said stiffly. "And now if you are ready, we will go in to my mother."

Janet wanted to ask so many questions, but he seemed to have closed a heavy door in her face. He had no intention of discussing the past, nor would he permit her to trespass across the threshold of the six years that had separated them.

Harriet looked up eagerly as they went into the room.

"Ah, there you are, Mark!" she greeted her son. "I thought I heard you with Jon in the paddock. It will be getting near his teatime, and Janet hasn't had anything to eat yet. She must be thirsty, at least, after her long journey. Has Heber put the kettle on?"

"I'm afraid Heber feels that he can ease up on the domestic chores now that we have a woman in the house to take over," Mark said, and Janet turned immediately.

"Of course," she agreed. "Let me get the tea. I've come to help as much as I can."

Mark watched her as she went out through the communicating door into the kitchen, making no attempt to follow her or show her around. He had told her that nothing at Wildfell was changed, and he would expect her to know her way around.

Certainly the kitchen was still the same, if you could except the limitations of a farmhand's efforts to clear up.

The grate was dull and the brass unpolished and there was what Harriet would have called a "tidemark" around the sink. The porcelain was broken, too, in places, and she wondered if it had ever occurred to Mark to replace it with something more modern. The open fireplace was another relic of the past that might justifiably have been labeled antiquated, but obviously it sufficed. Mark's wants were apparently few, and Harriet had never been one to question her lot while her husband was alive.

Perhaps they would come to the necessary improvements gradually, because she knew they existed at the Grange, and had done so for years.

Filling the kettle to make their tea, she remembered that there was no hot-water system in the house and put on a big, fire-blackened pot to heat while they ate their meal. She was struggling to the hob with it when Mark's shadow fell across the doorway, but he made no effort to help. A heavy silence hung between them when she had put the pot down.

"You'll soon fall into the old routine," he said at last. "Or would you like me to refresh your memory, Janet?"

"There's no need." Her voice sounded unfamiliar even in her own ears, strained and restricted. "I haven't forgotten, Mark."

"We take our dinner at noon and a supper at night," he explained. "There are 'lowens' for the field hands at eleven o'clock and again at three. You'll bake for these. The men expect a good meal when they come for the harvesting and again at the threshing. In the ordinary way there will only be Heber and the cowman and myself to cope with, apart from my mother and Jonathan."

He made the statement in a determined, unequivocal tone that brooked no argument on her part, and she felt that it had been long rehearsed.

"Very well, Mark," she agreed. "I haven't forgotten how to bake."

She remembered what had been known in the family as the baking days, three of them in one week, when mounds of scones and brown and white loaves had stood on the kitchen table beside the glistening Sally Lunns and the cookies bursting with currants. She remembered how Harriet Langdon would stand back, flushed and tired by her long morning in the heat of the big, stone-flagged kitchen, to admire her handiwork, and tried to imagine some of the satisfaction that the older woman must have felt, even when there was still the cleaning to be done and meals to be made and a mile or more, perhaps, to walk with the men's tea basket before three o'clock.

In those days there had been Ruth and herself to lend a hand, and then, suddenly, there had been no one but Harriet.

Remorse smote Janet anew. Why was youth so blind, she wondered, so that it had to learn from bitterest experience the ways of duty and love?

When the kettle had boiled she made the tea. Mark had produced eggs and a loaf that had been bought in Kirby Allerton two days ago.

"There's nothing else," he said. "We don't run to the niceties of cocktails before a meal at Wildfell. But perhaps you remember that, too?"

She set down the teapot and turned to face him, struggling with the hurt he seemed determined to inflict.

"Mark," she implored, "can't we start fair? If we have to live together it will be easier to live peaceably, don't you think? I'll make mistakes, but if you help me I'll soon fall back into the old routine. It is what I was brought up to do."

"But not what you wanted to do," he reminded her

evenly. "Why did you come back, Janet?" he demanded ruthlessly.

She could not tell him now. She had thought to meet the expected question with a confession of her continuing love and a plea for his forgiveness, but this cold, stern man was not the Mark she had known. He was what the past six years had made him, and no confession on her part, no plea for his clemency, would ever move him.

"I came because of your mother," she told him, supplying him with only half the truth. "I felt that she needed me."

"Which was generous of you, considering," he agreed. "We must see that you are sufficiently recompensed for your sacrifice."

Turning on his heel, he left her, and Janet stood staring down at the bubbling pan of water in which the eggs had been boiling for seven minutes.

Hurriedly she snatched it away from the heat, but the damage was already done. The eggs would be hard and unpalatable, but she could not keep Mark waiting while she boiled some more.

She carried them into the sitting room with an apology.

"I'm afraid the eggs are going to be harder than you like them," she said. "I—forgot about timing them."

Mark had set the round mahogany table near his mother's chair and covered it with a white linen cloth. It was worked with big yellow daisies, and Janet remembered embroidering it when she was at school. The sudden contact with the past made her look away from Harriet's kindly eyes. How long these old things lasted! Longer than love and fidelity, it seemed.

She put the tray down on the table and began to set out the cups and plates. Mark had not made any comment about the eggs.

"Call Jonathan," Harriet said. "He would stay out there all day with that pony of his!"

"When does he go to bed?" Janet asked.

"When he feels tired enough," Mark told her almost grudgingly. "Mostly he's out in the fields with me."

Janet wondered if this was going to be the first serious tussle between them. If he agreed to her return so that she would look after the child, she was determined to begin the task in the right way. A child of four should have a regular bedtime, and not just be allowed to wander the hillside till he grew too exhausted to protest any more. The issue could not be long delayed, she realized, as Jonathan bounced into the room.

"Go and wash your hands," Mark ordered. "And be quick about it, or your egg will be cold."

Janet grasped at the opportunity.

"Shall I boil him another one?"

Mark looked across at her, obviously surprised by the suggestion.

"We'll do with these," he said.

Jonathan came back almost immediately, presumably having wiped most of the dirt off on the towel that hung behind the kitchen door.

"This egg's hard!" he announced, striking the offending object with the back of his spoon without result. "It's like a dummy egg. Is it a dummy egg?" he demanded, looking suspiciously in Janet's direction. "Did she get it from under a broody hen?"

Mark looked down at his plate. He did not smile.

"No, Jonathan," he said. "The lady has forgotten how to boil eggs. Things will be better later on."

"Eat up your food and don't make such a fuss!" Harriet chided briskly. "Here! Put some butter in your egg now that you've got the top off. It will soften it."

Jonathan shot Janet an accusing look.

"I like my eggs soft," he complained.

"Tomorrow," Janet tried to say lightly, "you must help me in the kitchen, Jonathan. Would you like me to make you a gingerbread man?"

He considered her doubtfully.

"Will he be a hard man?"

"No," she said, laughing hollowly because she had wanted to say, "Not nearly so hard as your father has become!"

Mark left the table before they had finished their meal, with the excuse that he had to go to the Grange.

"Jonathan dawdles," he remarked. "He can find his own way across later."

Janet glanced pointedly at the clock. It was half-past five and four miles across the open moor to the Grange.

"Surely you will not allow him to go all that way alone?" she objected.

Level and demanding, Mark's eyes were instantly on hers.

"Why not? He can ride almost as well as I can."

"He is only four," she pointed out with equal determination. "He should have a recognized bedtime and not be allowed to ride about the moors of his own free will."

Mark strode to the door without answering, and Harriet sighed. Jonathan looked across the table into Janet's flushed face.

"You see, I *can* go," he said.

Janet bit her lip in exasperation.

"Finish your tea first," she advised not unkindly, "and then we'll see how late it is."

Harriet sat with her cup in her hand, gazing out of the window across the paddock, deep in her own thoughts, which she evidently would not voice before her grandson, and presently they saw Mark ride away, tall and straight in the saddle, a remote, stern figure, traversing the moor alone.

In some ways, Janet thought, even strong men could be weak. Mark was spoiling the child, of course, and it could only be out of devotion to Jonathan's mother. Mark must have loved her with an almost fanatical intensity that seemed to demand the rest of his life.

"You'll be tired, Janet," Harriet said, "after your long journey. I wish there was help for you in the house, but Martha Crosby isn't fit to come all this way, and there's work for the younger girls nearer at hand in the village. Mark won't have any of them living in."

"There's no need for that," Janet said. "Now that I've come back." She stood beside the table looking down at Harriet's graying head and the frail, almost useless hands clasping the blue cup. "I'll need your guidance, Mother Harriet," she added unsteadily. "And your help."

The faded gray eyes lifted to hers.

"You'll need patience, Janet," Hariet Langdon said, "more than anything else."

Janet tried to smile.

"I think that might be the most difficult part," she said.

Jonathan scraped back his chair.

"I'm going out," he announced.

Without looking at the clock again, Janet said, "I wish you wouldn't. You see, I'm not quite sure where everything is kept, and I'd like to heat a lot of water for your bath. Perhaps you could help me, Jonathan, just at first?"

Jonathan frowned, although part of her suggestion seemed to hold some sort of appeal for him.

"I know where to get the water," he said, "but my pony isn't tied up. Sometimes he runs away."

"Well, supposing we go out and tie him up, and then come back and fill the bath?"

He continued to frown doubtfully for a moment, thinking about the ride to the Grange.

"You can go to the Grange tomorrow," Harriet prompted, aware of strategy and near capitulation. "The reaper will be going over and you can ride on the tractor coming back."

Jonathan stifled a yawn.

"All right," he agreed. "I'll stay this time."

Janet piled the dishes onto the tray, and when she had tidied them onto a corner of the kitchen bench, they went in search of the pony. Jonathan was already tired, but he would not give in to sleep, insisting on a last ride around the paddock before they fastened the pony in for the night.

How like Mark he was, Janet thought, watching as he rode, straight backed, around the field, his small, determined chin thrust out, his hands brown and already capable on the rein. He had no fear and a strong will. The sort of will, she mused, that could ride to disaster.

Thrusting the disturbing thought from her, she helped him out of the saddle, although she realized that he could do it very well alone. His independence was fiercely assertive, as Mark's had always been. Father and son, she thought, with a stab of envy shooting through her that was very near to physical pain. The boy was obviously Mark's whole world now, so that there could be little room for anyone else.

When she had heated enough water in the big boiler that crouched in the darkest corner of the stone-flagged scullery, she carried it in pailfuls to the zinc bath that Jonathan had dragged from under the kitchen bench and set before the fire. The whole procedure might have struck her as completely primitive if she had not been able to shut out the memory of these intervening years when her own bathroom had been something she had come to expect. Taking a bath had been a matter of turning on a chromium-plated tap and luxuriating in perfumed ease till it pleased her to emerge refreshed into the air-conditioned atmosphere of a bedroom overlooking a warm blue sea. Yet, in less than no time, it seemed, she had turned back the years and did not feel it strange to be adapting herself to the old conditions so swiftly.

It did occur to her that Mark, in his present financial circumstances, could very well have afforded a bathroom and a hot-water system at Wildfell, but she did not think to question his decision. It was fun, she considered, to bath Jonathan before the kitchen fire.

Kneeling on the hearth rug, she felt the years slipping away, and her laughter, mingling with the child's was that of a happy girl again. Jonathan, having shed his first suspicion of her and most of his initial shyness, shrieked at the top of his voice, so that neither heard the heavy footstep on the uncarpeted boards of the house until Mark stood looking at them.

"Look!" Jonathan exclaimed, holding up a handful of soapsuds for his inspection. "Froth!"

Janet pushed a fallen strand of hair back from her brow with a wet forearm. She had put on one of Harriet's overalls and her cheeks were flushed from the warmth of the fire and her exertions. She turned slowly to look at Mark, drawing in her breath in an involuntary gasp at the change in his expression. His face had gone gray beneath its coating of tan and his handsome mouth was twisted into a bitter line, while above it the eyes, which so short a time ago had reflected nothing but cynicism, held a look of suppressed agony from which she turned almost in self-defense.

Something had torn away the barrier to the past, opening up the floodgates of his despair, and she knew that she had not been meant to see. The domestic scene, for which he had been wholly unprepared, had caught him off guard, plunging him back among his memories, and he must have seen her kneeling there, as Jonathan's mother would have knelt in happier circumstances.

"I don't want to come out!" Jonathan chanted. "I don't want to go to bed!"

Numbed by the silent encounter, Janet waited for Mark to speak.

"You'd better do as you are told," he said quietly after the barest of pauses. "It's almost seven o'clock."

Janet wrapped the child in a towel, reaching down his pajamas from the rail above the hob where she had put them to warm. Already there was an autumnal nip in the air on this high ridge of the moor, and she remembered the chill of the big raftered bedrooms from her own childhood.

"Carry me! Carry me!" Jonathan demanded when he saw Mark about to leave them. "You always do."

For an instant Mark hesitated, and then he swung the child up to his shoulder and turned toward the stairs.

"Have you said good-night to your grandmother, Jonathan?" Janet asked.

"No. I'll say it now."

Janet did not accompany them to Harriet's room. She stayed behind in the kitchen, fighting back an emotion that was almost as strong as Mark's had been. She had no real part in all this, although in some strange way Mark seemed to find her necessary in his scheme of things. Anyone else would have done as well, perhaps, she told herself bitterly, some stranger with the mother instinct necessary to bring up his son.

When he came out of the sitting room still perched on Mark's shoulder, Jonathan held out a hand to her.

"You come, too," he invited.

"I'm going to empty your bath."

"No," he persisted. "I want you to come."

Mark did not speak, and she followed them up the stairs, feeling guilty of renewing the agony she had surprised in his eyes in that unguarded moment in the kitchen. Why had he come back? What, she wondered desperately, had brought him from the Grange before Jonathan was safely in bed and asleep? Could it have been anxiety for the boy riding alone across the moor, although he had expressed absolute confidence in his safety?

She stood by the bed, wondering if the child had been taught to say his prayers, and presently Jonathan screwed up his face and mumbled something unintelligible, which seemed to pass with Mark. He then promptly buried his head beneath the blankets and announced that he was a mole.

"No more fun and games!" Mark admonished, slapping the mole on his bottom. "Time to go to sleep."

Jonathan's head appeared and he surveyed them with one eye, deciding after a moment that the voice of authority had spoken at last.

Mark turned toward the door.

For an instant Janet hesitated. She wanted to kiss the child's smooth forehead under its shock of red gold hair, but she could not hurt Mark further.

"Good night, Jon!" she said. "See you in the morning!"

Mark closed the bedroom door behind them. In the narrow passageway she had to wait for him to move.

"First blood, Janet," he said. "You managed it very cleverly."

She turned impulsively.

"I wish we didn't have to scrap like this, Mark," she whispered. "About Jonathan or —anything else."

His mouth, in the half darkness of the unlit passage, looked almost cruel.

"Perhaps it is in the nature of things that we should differ," he said briefly, standing aside to let her pass and defeating further argument.

Shaken and disconcerted, Janet paused at the living-room door.

"When does your mother go to bed?" she asked.

"Generally about this time. I'm afraid she needs a certain amount of help."

Janet dismissed the unwashed tea things and the bath of water on the kitchen floor. The truth was that she had never felt so tired before. The emotional strain of her meeting with Mark Langdon had begun to show on her face and she had been traveling from early morning. She ran a hand through her fine, soft hair as she went into the sitting room, a trick she had had as a child when she felt unsure and alone.

Harriet Langdon saw it, and her eyes darkened with misgiving.

"Don't let Mark break your spirit, Janet," she said unexpectedly. "He's changed so much in these past six years that sometimes even I hardly know him."

"His grief has gone very deep," Janet answered in a tone that seemed almost frigid. "I hope that he does not think that I mean to interfere too much between him and Jonathan."

"If he thought that," Harriet said heavily, "he would send you away."

For the first time Janet realized how completely Mark had become master at Wildfell, and her own position there seemed all the more precarious in consequence. He had said, however, that his mother needed her care and companionship, and she believed it to be true.

Apart from that strange, almost forced reserve that she had noticed from the beginning, Harriet Langdon had accepted her on the old footing of a daughter in the house, and as she helped her into the adjoining room and made her comfortable for the night, Janet felt more grateful for that acceptance than for anything else. If she had wronged Harriet by going away, at least she had been forgiven, generously and completely.

"Mark will need a bite to eat before he goes to bed," Harriet suggested apologetically as she crossed to the door. "And Heber won't be willing to get his own meals now that you're here to cook for them."

"I'll see what I can do," Janet promised brightly, although she was almost dropping with fatigue.

It had taken her over an hour to get Harriet to bed, to give her a bed bath and draw the thick hair back from the high forehead that was so like Mark's, so that it could be braided into two plaits for the night, but the extra effort had been well worthwhile. Harriet had sunk back on her pillows with a contented sigh, saying that she had never felt so well cared for in her life.

The sight of those thin, frail hands distressed Janet when she remembered them so well as the hard brown working hands of a vigorous countrywoman. Now Harriet Langdon was like a child, utterly dependent and a little afraid.

"You will stay?" she had begged almost piteously when Janet had stooped to tuck in the last blanket and turn out the lamp.

"Yes," Janet had promised, "I'll stay for as long as you need me."

But in the kitchen she wondered why she had felt so confident. She knew deep in her heart that Mark Langdon had the power to make her life as uncomfortable as he chose and that he would not hesitate to dismiss her as bluntly as he had bidden her come. There was no guarantee that she would remain there. She had appealed to him twice in four hours, to be met with a cold hostility that had chilled her to the bone. He was not willing to meet her even halfway or make any pretense at friendship when he could feel nothing for her but a deepening contempt.

The tasks he had assigned to her were nothing. She would have done them all, and more, joyfully, if she could have come to them by some happier way.

Someone had lifted the bath from the hearth and emptied the water into the sink. Heber, she imagined, by the amount that had been slopped across the floor in the process, but she had no way of telling whether or not Mark had given the order.

Kneeling down, she began to mop up the surplus water from the rough stone flags, and when she had finished she washed up the dishes and looked around for something to prepare for Mark's supper.

The men were still out in the fields at the Grange, and Mark with them. There was only the cowman left at Wildfell, and he slouched about in the yard outside, muttering to himself. It had been wet for several days and he left a trail of mud behind him wherever he went, bringing it with him into the houseplace and into the kitchen and scullery when he came to answer some question of Janet's.

She wondered how long Mark would be. She had found some cold mutton in the pantry and a cheese that had been freshly cut, and she put them out on the table. Then, for the first time, she wondered how they would take their meal. Heber and the cowman in the kitchen before the bright fire she had built up, and Mark and herself in the sitting room beyond?

Suddenly her hands began to tremble. Being flung into so intimate a contact with the one man who was her life, knowing so well that his love for her had died long since, was too cruel. She could not face him across the homely board with the realization in her heart that she would never reach him no matter how hard she tried.

To go to bed before her final tasks were done might be considered defeat, however, and suddenly she knew that Mark Langdon wanted to see her defeated.

She drew in a deep breath and turned back to the fire.

At ten o'clock Heber came in, followed by the silent cowman. She set their food before them, thanking Heber for emptying the bath.

"T' maister told me as I had to do it. It is a flaysome job for a woman," Heber informed her grudgingly.

Janet wondered why the remark should have surprised her when she was already half-aware that Mark would go out of his way to give her the most difficult, even the menial tasks about the farm, taking an almost sadistic delight in her efforts to do them to his liking. She was forced to remember that these were the tasks she had scorned six years ago when she had left Wildfell, rejecting Mark's love for the fuller life she had hoped to find in the south.

Carrying their supper into the adjoining room and kneeling to stir the wood fire into a blaze, she knew that these six years had changed her. The girl who had wanted life to be easy and adventurous was now a woman, deeply in love.

The warmth of the inner room enfolded her, but still Mark did not come. She waited, but the clock ticking softly on the high mantelpiece above her head was the only sound disturbing the silence of the night.

Outside it had grown quite dark. There was no moon, but she did not light the lamps because the fire was still bright. It seemed that she had waited for an eternity when she heard Heber and the cowman crossing the yard to their own quarters, but still there was no sign of Mark.

Nervously she poured herself a cup of tea, deciding to

make a fresh potful when Mark came. The silence deepened and the ticking clock hammered a mocking refrain in her brain.

"*First blood, Janet. First blood! You managed it very well.*"

She was asleep when he found her and the clock was striking two.

"There was no need for you to wait up," he said harshly. The mark of rain was on his coat and his hair was wet, as if he had been riding a long way across the moor. "I can fend for myself at this hour."

His voice had sounded thick, and she could not see his face clearly because the fire had died into pale ash in the grate, but he looked as if he had been standing there for some minutes, and his mouth was as bitterly grim as it had been when he had come across her bathing Jonathan before the kitchen fire.

Unsteadily she rose to her feet.

"I'll make you some fresh tea."

"No," he said, turning to the fire. "Go to bed."

Her hands trembling, she lifted the cold teapot, carrying it through the kitchen where she raked the ashes in the deep well of the grate to a swift, fierce blaze. The kettle, standing on the warm hob, had boiled again even before she had finished clearing away the remnants of the meal that she had prepared for Heber and the cowman, and she poured the scalding water over the fresh tea leaves with the bitterness of gall in her heart. It would always be like this. Always her efforts turned aside with contempt and indifference.

When she turned Mark was standing in the doorway between the two rooms, looking at her.

"I told you not to do that," he said. "When I come in at this hour I can look after myself."

"It's my work," she said unevenly. Her brief sleep had

not refreshed her, and a weighted tiredness pressed heavily against her lids. "I made a meal already, expecting you earlier."

He did not answer her. The silence between them became fraught with a danger that a spark might set alight instantly. They could not live like this, Janet thought desperately. They could not go on pushing up barriers for ever.

"Would it not have been easier for you to send for Ruth?" she asked unhappily.

Mark's eyes darkened to a fury of anger, but when he spoke his voice was coolly controlled.

"Ruth does not come into this," he said. "If you remember, it was you who asked to come back, Janet."

Yes, she remembered. She remembered the eagerness with which she had flown across half a continent to return to the scene of their love; she remembered her plans and her pitiful little hopes for forgiveness, and saw them lying as dead and gray as the ash at her feet.

Blindly she began to stack the china in the rack above the sink, setting the table for an early-morning meal before she made her way into the hall by the far door instead of going through the sitting room again. But the sitting-room door was open and Mark lifted the lamp from the table and followed her to the foot of the stairs.

"You'll need this," he said harshly, "to see your way."

Her way in the dark? He held the lamp out to her and its light flared suddenly in his eyes. They were deep wells of pain, and she took the lamp from him, as if to obliterate it.

"Good night, Mark," she said.

When she reached her bedroom she closed the door, leaning heavily against it, her heart thudding as if she had been running. In her tired state her mind refused to function properly and it was several minutes before she set the lamp down on the table beside the window.

Curtains were rarely drawn at Wildfell, and she stared out into the darkness of a night devoid of stars. It was so dark that she could not even see the familiar outline of the farm buildings across the yard, and the silence of the moor seemed to press in upon her like a heavy hand.

She stood like that for a long time, hardly thinking, until Jonathan, crying out in the room next door, took her into the corridor to listen. The child's door was ajar, and after a minute all was still. Something had disturbed him in his sleep, some aspect of his busy day returning to puzzle and bewilder him in dreams. She opened his door a fraction wider, standing just inside the room to assure herself that he had turned over and was now deeply, dreamlessly asleep, and after a minute or two the soft, regular breathing contented her.

She waited a moment longer, feeling the warmth and nearness of the child, until a movement in the adjoining room set her pulses racing and closed a strangling hand about her throat.

Swiftly she realized that it had been there all the time, the dulled sound of a man's regular pacing up and down, up and down, the torture of his memories allowing him no respite and dismissing sleep.

Without being told, she knew that it was Mark's room.

CHAPTER TWO

THERE WAS MUCH to be done during the next few days because the reapers were out in the Grange fields, and Janet scarcely seemed to see Harriet at all.

"We'll plan a routine," she had suggested on the first morning, "so that we can have five minutes to ourselves now and then," but somehow the routine had been swallowed up in extra domestic chores and they had not even had time to talk.

Her first baking day had been a nightmare to Janet. The weather had turned warm again, with all the promise of a lush Indian summer in the heat of the sun, and the great farmhouse kitchen was close and stuffy in consequence. Baking over an open fire had left her flushed and enervated, but there was a deep satisfaction in her eyes when her work was done. If some of her scones were sadly misshapen and it was not exactly Harriet's kind of bread that adorned the wide dresser by noon, at least she did not need to hang her head in abject failure.

Mark did not notice these things, but there was a sense of achievement in her own heart.

Heber had taken the first "lowens" down to the fields, but on the second day, having organized the housework so that she need not spend every moment of her time scrubbing and tidying, she packed the tea basket and decided to walk to the Grange with it for three o'clock.

Harriet slept in the afternoon, and Jonathan had gone

off with Mark first thing in the morning, carrying a packed lunch and some fruit.

Curiosity about the Grange kept her thoughts busy as she walked across the moor, and after the first mile she could see the reapers at work far beneath her in the Grange fields. It was a glorious day of wind and sun, and her spirits rose to a strange excitement as she felt the warmth and freshness of it on her face. This was her country, as it was Mark's. It might have taken her six years and the wilting panorama of the Alpine foothills to release it, but she was sure of it at last.

She lifted her face to the breeze, feeling it blowing through her loosened hair with a new contentment, her heart lighter than it had been for days. Somehow, some-time, she and Mark might be able to resolve their differences, because they could not live together in such close prox-imity and remain enemies.

If the memory of Mark's eyes on that first evening gave the lie to such a hope, she crushed the conviction down. On such a day there was little room for fear.

Jonathan hailed her from the back of the tractor. He was perched up behind one of the Grange men, flushed and excited by the adventure of bumping around a twenty-acre field with the huge blades of the reaper swish-ing behind him and tossing the sheaves out at intervals on its way.

The scene at Scarton Grange was as different from that at Wildfell as it was possible to imagine. Deep in the green heart of the dale, on its western and more sheltered side, the rich, pro-ductive soil of Scarton offered a harvest that any farmer might well have envied, and when she saw Mark standing at the edge of the field, idle for a moment as he scrutinized his handiwork, she wondered what special brand of satisfaction it gave him to stand there, owner of all he surveyed.

The merging of the two farms had come as a complete surprise to her. It had been Matthew Langdon's lifelong ambition to own more productive land than he had at Wildfell, and he had made an enemy of Clive Ransome because the owner of Scarton Grange had refused him even an acre or two. Harsh and unforgiving over what he considered an injury, he had forbidden Clive Ransome's son to come within a mile of Wildfell, yet Tom Ransome and Ruth had met inevitably at Young Farmers' dances and on their separate ways about the dale.

"Mark," Janet asked when she had put her basket down, "what became of the Ransomes? I know the old man died shortly after I left, but—Tom? He was so fond of Scarton. It was in his blood."

"If it was, his blood was thin. He sold out very easily."

The brief, unsympathetic answer reminded her so much of his father that she looked up at him in surprise.

"What happened?" she asked.

"He found himself short of money." He shrugged expressively. "And I happened to have enough to buy him out."

"I can't imagine Tom giving up the Grange easily," Janet said after a most awkward pause. "Surely there was something he could have done to keep it in Ransome hands after four generations?"

"Apparently not." Mark's lips were thin, his eyes darkened to an undefinable color as he looked down toward the Grange. "Tom Ransome has no part in the life here now," he added harshly. "We never speak of him. The Grange is Langdon land now, and it's up to me to see that it doesn't suffer from its sudden change of ownership."

She could not remember this harshness in Mark nor could she argue against it as she might have done six years ago. He had built so many barriers around himself that she could not attempt to scale even the first of them, and she was almost glad when they were joined by the farm manager from the Grange. He had been the Ransomes' foreman for years, a small, wiry man in his late forties, who seemed impressed by his unexpected promotion. He was a hard worker and a good judge of livestock, and she was sure that he would amply repay Mark's trust in him.

Otherwise, she thought, as they shook hands, he would not be there very long.

"It's nice to see you again, miss," he said respectfully. "It will be a grand thing for Mrs. Langdon to have you back home."

Janet smiled, feeling absurdly grateful for his welcome. The kindly smile and firm handshake made up in some small way for Mark's coldness and his uncommunicative attitude about the Grange, but the word "home" had a changed meaning for her now.

As was expected of him, "the master" took his tea with her, a little way apart from the hired men who sat in the shade with their backs against the newly stacked ricks. He did not eat anything, drinking his tea as quickly as possible, obviously impatient to start work again, although it did not look as if the weather would break before the oats were safely stored under cover in the Scarton barns. These fine spells often lasted for days when they came, sometimes even for weeks, and then the dale was the loveliest spot on earth, with its deeply shadowed sides and the stocked grain lying in the narrow trough of sunlight at its foot.

Scarton Creek—or the "beck," as they called it—ran through the Grange fields. Janet watched it shimmering in the sun as Mark stood beside her, chafing with impatience.

"I've thought of the beck so often, Mark, these past six years," she said, without quite knowing why she should try to share her thoughts with the stranger he had become. "It has a voice of its own that one can never forget."

"Even with the noisy clamor of the Mediterranean sounding in your ears, Janet? I thought that would have shut out all other sound."

He was trying to hurt her, but today she would not let him succeed.

"Not if it is truly part of you," she said. "One never really forgets one's childhood and the things that matter most."

He made a swift gesture of dissent.

"That may be the nostalgic view," he argued, "but it isn't practicable. We must move with the times and our own inclinations."

"Which means that you think people change—inevitably?" she challenged in a choked undertone. "It isn't invariably true, Mark."

"No?" He looked unconvinced. "I'm sorry I can't agree with that, and aren't we told that change is a good thing?"

"It depends on—how one changes," she answered with difficulty.

He appeared to have nothing to say to that, filling his pipe and stuffing the tobacco hard down into the bowl as if he would drive home a conviction that he had long held in his own mind.

Janet got to her feet with a sigh.

"Time to be going back," she said regretfully. "I've loved coming down here into the sunshine and warmth. The Grange was always such a friendly spot."

"There have been changes there, too," he reminded her dryly. "I'm afraid you would find it almost as bleak and deserted as Wildfell now."

He had not invited her to go to the house, although she had been there many times in the past. Perhaps he considered that old memories were best left undisturbed. Old and more pleasant memories.

"Do you wish me to take Jonathan back with me?" she asked as he prepared to join the workers in the field.

"I doubt if he'll go while the reaper's in action," Mark said, looking across the yellow stubble to where the child stood expectantly beside the tractor. "He's a farmer born and bred."

His mouth was thinly compressed and he seemed to find little joy in the remark, although there could be no doubt about the fact that he was bringing up the boy to take a pride in the land that would be his one day. All of Wildfell and all of Scarton rolled into one, as Mark now saw it because of his own effort.

Fate had been kind to him in that respect, Janet thought as she turned away. What else *did* Mark want?

Before there could be any hope of any answer to her unspoken question, a child's sharp cry pierced the air. She turned and saw Mark running, vaulting the fence that separated them from the field in one bound and crashing down across the stubble to where the reaper had ceased to turn. The silence as the heavy blades stopped revolving could almost be felt, and then she was running blindly herself, stumbling over the rutted surface of the field towards the group of workmen gathered about the tractor.

Mark was brushing Jonathan down. He had apparently been struck a glancing blow by one of the heavy blades and thrown forward onto his face. Well away from the danger zone, thank God! Janet pushed through the silent group with the thankful prayer in her heart. There was probably no real harm done, but Jonathan would be shaken and frightened by the unexpected experience.

As soon as he saw her he burst into tears.

"It hit me!" he wailed, although he had kept a stiff upper lip while Mark had him in hand. "The naughty reaper hit me!"

"All right! Let me see." She held out her arms to him and he ran to her immediately, ignoring Mark in the softer atmosphere of a woman's sympathy. "Have you been hurt much? There isn't anything to see, is there? Perhaps it was only the poor old reaper's way of being playful when you went so near. They're clumsy things, you know. I once knew a reaper who did those things on purpose because it didn't like little boys touching its blades."

The men smiled and returned to their work, thankful that no serious damage had been done, but Mark stood his ground, staring down at them as if he resented Janet's interference.

"I didn't touch it," Jonathan protested, near to tears again. "It just hit me when I wanted to get on the tractor. I don't like reapers, and it hurt my hand!"

His hand and arm were grazed, but not badly. Janet took out her handkerchief.

"We'll go down to the beck and wash your hand, shall we?" she suggested, picking him up in her arms. "It isn't very far. Only to the bottom of the field."

Jonathan allowed her to carry him, locking his arms firmly about her neck, and when the grazed hand had been duly bathed he looked up at her mournfully.

"You wouldn't have done that to me, would you?" he demanded in a hurt voice.

Janet saw that he was still deeply shaken and she gathered him into her arms.

"Don't coddle the child!"

She had not seen Mark coming down across the field toward them, and she started at the sound of his voice until anger at its harshness canceled out all other emotion.

"Mark, he has been hurt!" she protested.

"It's nothing serious," he told her almost curtly. "He will have to be toughened early if he is not to be hurt a great deal more later on."

Jonathan slid from Janet's knee, standing uncertainly between them for a moment before he ran off to lean over the stone coping of the little humpbacked bridge that spanned the stream.

"Why are you so inhuman?" Janet demanded, meeting Mark's eyes with a fiery accusation in her own. "He was more frightened than hurt, but it's the same thing."

"Am I inhuman?" His eyes remained gray and level on hers with no indication of his true feelings in their depths. "I don't think so, Janet. Shall we say I learned my own lesson in a hard school?"

He meant the past; he meant that she had played her part in these things, but she could not hold herself fully responsible for all his present bitterness.

Had he, she wondered, lost or parted with his wife in some tragic circumstances that he would not allow himself to forget? His devotion to Jonathan suggested it, yet he seemed relentless in his pursuit of a way of life that might spoil the child's future and darken his own.

She did not really want to think of Jonathan's mother, envying her because she had given Mark what she herself had denied him. She did not even know if Mark's wife was still alive. He had kept the past a closed book, even from his mother, and it was not likely that he would unburden himself to her.

"Jonathan will probably go home with you now,"

Mark said. "Though he'll want to go by the road and take the pony."

"Do you think he should ride all that way?"

"I think so."

The decision was clear-cut and decisive, and she did not argue.

"You'll have to walk up to the Grange," he explained. "We stable the pony there, out of the sun."

Surprisingly he went with them, over the home meadows and through the fir plantation that skirted the road. Under the trees it was cool and dark and vaguely intimate, and Janet felt that she could have walked like this with Mark all her life.

"We'll have to get a bathroom put in at Wildfell," he said, "now that Jonathan is getting older. I've had very little time to think of these things in the past few months."

"We could do with hot water," she agreed, "and a bathroom's a necessity these days."

He looked up at the four stout walls of Scarton Grange as they came upon it, suddenly, through the trees.

"It's all there, including the trimmings," he said. "It's a pity it will never be occupied."

Had he meant to live there with Jonathan's mother, when he had first bought it? The question pierced through Janet with all the cruelty of a rapier thrust, and the fact that Mark made no attempt to enter the house itself intensified the impression in her mind. Scarton Grange would have made him a gracious home, with its long, south-facing windows overlooking the dale and the winding beck flowing gently through its garden, making deep brown pools between the gray rockery stones and tumbling in miniature falls to the level of the fields.

Yet it stood empty and deserted but for the few rooms

taken over by the manager and his wife, and Mark had just said that it would remain so.

"I bought it as it stood," he explained when they were near enough to see the curtains drawn back from the windows and the dim shape of the heavy furniture in the lower rooms. "That was how Ransome wanted to sell."

She knew that he would not make any further effort to enlighten her over the terms of the sale, but she felt that she understood why Tom Ransome had wanted his old home to remain as it was.

Jonathan decided to ride the pony, and Mark helped him into the saddle.

"I don't suppose you'll be home for a meal before sunset?" Janet asked. "You work a long day, Mark."

"I may not even be home then," he said indifferently. "Don't wait for me."

His comings and goings were to be none of her concern, Janet realized with a heavy heart. They were to remain as far apart in the future as they had been on that first day of her arrival at Wildfell.

Lingeringly her eyes dwelt on the long windows of the Grange as Mark strode away through the wood and back to the fields where he was reaping his first harvest in bitterness and regret. Would he ever come to look on the Grange as his true home and accept its happiness and peace?

"Come on!" Jonathan urged, drawing on the rein. "We've got a long way to go."

They were halfway to Wildfell when a car appeared on the horizon, a small open two-seater that had seen better days.

Vaguely Janet seemed to recognize it, and when it drew up on the narrow road to let the pony pass, she looked through the windshield into a pair of brown eyes that returned her scrutiny without hesitation.

"I thought it couldn't be anyone but you, Janet!" Tom Ransome said as he swung his long legs over the low door and stood looking down at her with his old, friendly smile. "You haven't changed much, have you? A bit thinner, perhaps, and more sophisticated, but the dale will soon put that right!"

"I wouldn't say that you had changed, either!" Janet laughed, holding out her hand with a pitiful sort of eagerness for friendship that he was quick to see. "It's lovely to meet you again."

"And unexpected, I should say?" He sent a fleeting glance down into the dale, where the tall chimneys of Scarton Grange were still visible above the trees. "Have you been to Scarton?"

"Only to the fields." She felt uneasy, afraid that she might be opening an old wound, one that surely could not have had time to heal. "They're harvesting down there and I've been over with their tea."

"It's old history," he said, guessing her embarrassment. "Don't worry about it, Janet." His eyes were friendly and warm. "I've almost got used to the idea of being without Scarton these days, and I don't think there's anyone I'd rather see there than Mark."

It was impossible to hide her surprise, and to cover her confusion a little she turned to the child who had brought his pony round to her side.

"This is Jonathan," she introduced them. "Mark's boy."

"Yes," Tom said, "I heard Mark had come back with a son. Mark's changed in a good many ways, Janet, but he seems to be devoted to this little fellow, at least." He stooped to fondle the pony's nose, looking up at the boy in the saddle with a suggestion of regret in his friendly smile. "Jonathan, eh?" he said. "A big name for a small boy. But perhaps they call you Jon?"

Jonathan shook his head in emphatic denial.

"Men don't only ladies. My pony's name is Rusty," he volunteered companionably in the next breath in answer to Tom's friendly smile.

"And you found him at the Grange?" Tom suggested. "Shall I let you into a secret? I used to ride him when I was young. He must be all of twenty years old."

There was no resentment in him, Janet realized. He had sold his old home and Mark had bought it, lock, stock and barrel. That was all. It had been a fair deal and Tom Ransome had never been one to harbor a grudge.

Not like Mark. Janet felt her heart contract with pain as she remembered how Mark had looked when she had mentioned Tom.

"Are you on your way to the Grange?" she asked unsteadily.

Tom shook his head.

"No. I'm just passing through the dale." He seemed to hesitate, as if he was not quite sure how much she knew. "I've a notion to come back, Janet, though, not to Scarton. I'm trying my hand in a small way on the other side of the fell."

She looked at him doubtfully, seeing a shadow in his eyes that had not been there before.

"Will that answer?" she asked. "So near to the Grange?"

"I can't be quite sure," he confessed, "till I've tried it. When I saw this small piece of land at Kirby Allerton advertised in the *Journal*, I felt that I had to come. I can't try to explain it," he added with his eyes on the distant hills. "It was just there."

"I think I know what you mean," Janet said. "It was the same sort of conviction that brought me back to Wildfell."

He regarded her steadily for a moment without speaking and then he said, "I thought you would understand how it was. Whether it will work out for me or not remains to be seen."

He had taken it for granted that things were working out right for her, Janet thought, smiling wistfully at the suggestion. Her old liking for Tom Ransome had been renewed by this meeting, yet it seemed that he, also, was subtly changed. The past six years had aged him considerably. He could not be any more than thirty, yet there were flecks of gray in his hair, fading little patches above the temples that suggested he might be a man with a burden.

The loss of Scarton could have put those telltale gray hairs there, of course, but somehow she had the feeling that it was not Scarton alone that had aged him. Something had reached right down into the depths of the man and scarred him deeply.

"I hope we're going to meet again," he said sincerely when he finally stepped aside to let them pass. "The other side of the fell isn't so far away, Janet. In fact it's almost nearer to Wildfell than to the Grange."

After she had turned away Janet wondered why neither of them had mentioned Ruth. In the old days, Ruth's name would have cropped up between them inevitably, but Tom seemed to have forgotten Ruth. Had he forgotten his old love for her, too?

She pondered the question all the way back to Wildfell.

"I met Tom Ransome in the dale," she told Harriet, because Tom was very much in her mind. "He didn't look so very much different. A little older, perhaps. He's come back to try his hand at farming again over at Kirby Allerton."

Harriet was immediately interested.

"I never did understand why Tom left the dale," she

mused. "I often wonder if it was Matthew's attitude to him and Ruth that took him off to London without warning." She sat for a moment or two gazing down into the heart of the fire. "He was a stern man, was Matthew," she sighed. "Never relenting, never forgiving a wrong, if he chose to consider it as such. But he had no right to interfere with young people's lives. The old never have. When they have lived their own lives and made their own mistakes they ought to have a broader vision. Matthew's vision was always narrow," she concluded heavily, "but nobody could convince him that what he was doing wasn't right."

It was the longest speech Janet had ever heard from Harriet and the first time she had ever criticized her life's partner, alive or dead. Harriet Langdon believed that there was a respect due to marriage that open criticism undermined and she was loyal and forgiving in the extreme.

Janet put an arm around her thin shoulders.

"I believe Ruth would come home if Mark asked her," she said, but Harriet shook her head.

"She went away very quietly," she said, "without so much as a goodbye. She left Mark to say it for her. Maybe she thought it would upset me too much when I had been ill, but it was a strange thing for Ruth to do. When she was in London and her father forbade her to come back to Wildfell she wrote to me regularly, and even now I get a letter every so often telling me she's well." She let her head fall back against Janet's supporting arm, and it was no weight at all. "I'll never be able to feel that she's really happy in Canada," she added. "I've never felt that Ruth could settle down so far away from the dale."

"Does she know her father is dead?" Janet asked.

"Yes. Mark wrote and told her. They've never lost touch with one another."

Janet was glad of that, and she wondered if Mark would give her Ruth's address so that she, too, could write to Canada.

It was not until she had met Tom Ransome for a second time, however, that she remembered to ask Mark about Ruth.

The household tasks that had been neglected since Martha Crosby had stopped coming to Wildfell took up all her time during the next two weeks, but she was proud enough of the change she had made when she surveyed the well-scrubbed houseplace and Harriet's sitting room with its freshly laundered chair covers and clean curtains.

The good weather had held, and Mark had most of the harvest in at the Grange. There was nothing to gather at Wildfell, where he concentrated on sheep as the chief means of their livelihood, although the Wildfell wool crop could not mean the difference between comfort and near poverty that it had done in the past, now that the Grange was theirs as well.

Janet had not been able to take full advantage of the last of these sunny days in the way she would have wished, walking outdoors across the moor with the sun and wind in her face. There had been too much to do inside the house, and at times, when night came, she had been almost too tired to sleep. The routine work was never ending, yet she would not complain or ask Mark for help. Perhaps it was because she knew, somewhere deep down within her, that it would give him a savage sort of satisfaction to see her rise in revolt against the work she had begged him to let her do again. Perhaps he even wanted to prove to her—or himself—that she was incapable of doing it, that the past six years had softened her beyond endurance.

"You ought to get out," Harriet said at the end of the

second week. "Even if it's only for a walk across the moor. You could take a bicycle and go as far as Kirby Allerton and put in the grocery order at Musgrove's."

Heber had mended Ruth's old bicycle for his own use, parting with it grudgingly when Janet asked if she might borrow it, but she had never been out on it until now.

She wheeled it across the yard and pumped up the tires. Now that the reaper was out of action, Jonathan had gone to ride on the grain wagon on its trips between the fields and the Grange, and Harriet would sleep the afternoon away, nodding peacefully on her couch beside the window, which Janet had closed because the sun had gone in.

The wind was colder as she pushed the bicycle on to the narrow moor road, and there was a dampness in the air blowing in from the sea. Mark's spell of fine weather was all but over, but he would not mind when it had achieved the results he had wanted. The harvest at the Grange was home.

Instinctively she knew that there would not be any celebration of the fact, as there had been in former years when Clive Ransome was master there. There would be no Harvest Home, with its lavish supper and merry punch bowl, which dated back to more spacious times when the whole dale was one vast estate and the lord of the manor had entertained his tenant farmers at Scarton Grange. Mark had closed that chapter in the dale's history with a firm hand and there was no one to question his right.

She had hardly seen Mark during the past three days and when she had remarked on an undisturbed bed Heber had explained that "t'maister would have slept at t'Grange, as like as not."

The thought disturbed her, but she knew that she could

not question Mark's movements. She had no right. If he chose to sleep at the Grange, nothing she could say would induce him to come home.

Only Jonathan could do that. His fondness for the child was the one softening element in his life. It never varied and his indulgences increased. Janet realized that if she were to interfere at every point where their ideas about the boy's upbringing clashed she would be eternally at war with Mark.

Cycling along the ridge in the shadow of the fell, she found herself thinking about Ruth, and was not, therefore, greatly surprised to stumble upon Tom Ransome coming out of the post office at Kirby Allerton with an armful of groceries and two letters in his hand.

"Wait till I've posted these and then we'll talk!" Tom greeted her. "I've been wondering when I would catch up with you Janet."

"I'm on a shopping spree," she told him with a laugh. "I'm even tempted to wait and go to the movies!"

"You can't," he pointed out, slipping his letters into the maw of the box in the wall. "It's Thursday, and they only function on Tuesdays and Saturdays."

"Bad luck!" Janet smiled. "I don't suppose I would really have gone, even if I had had the chance," she added. "It's quite a way back to Wildfell, and it's getting dark earlier these days."

He glanced at his watch.

"It's not much after four. Come out and see the new Ransome effort and have a cup of tea," he invited. "I have acquired a housekeeper and a dog, and the chickens have just arrived!"

"Is that the new effort?" she asked, immediately interested. "Eggs?"

"Eggs and dressed poultry and, later on, a few pedigree pigs."

"How far out are you?" she asked doubtfully. The harvest's home, and Mark may be back for tea."

"Hang Mark and his tea for once!" he suggested recklessly "I'd like you to see the bungalow and tell me what you think of it."

It was impossible to refuse, to disappoint him. He looked younger and a little more happy today, Janet thought, with only the faintest shadow in his eyes, the merest hint that life might not have been too kind to him in the past.

"All right, I'll come," she agreed. "But what can I possibly do with my bike?"

"You can ride it behind me," he instructed. "It's no more than a quarter of a mile to the bungalow and I'll go slowly."

The two-seater was parked a little way along the road, with a sack of corn and some other feeding stuff in the passenger's seat, so that it would have been next to impossible to offer her a lift, in any case.

"A typical farmer's car!" she laughed. "Are you sure your housekeeper will relish the idea of a visitor at such short notice, by the way?"

"Don't worry about that," he called over his shoulder. "She's a treasure without price!"

The treasure without price was feeding the hens when they arrived, but she put down her pail as they drew up and came down across the field toward them.

"Mrs. Bowes," Tom said, "this is a very old friend of mine. Do you think you could get her a cup of tea?"

The tea was prepared while Tom took Janet around the property to inspect chicken coops and newly laid-out runs while he explained the improvements he hoped to make before the year was out.

The bungalow itself was small but compact, quite big

enough for two people, and there was plenty of ground attached to it for Tom's modest ambitions to thrive.

When she rose to go, Janet felt genuine regret, but the clock on the mantelpiece said six and she had already stayed too long.

"If you're really worrying about getting back before it's dark, you could go by Parson's Crag," Tom suggested. "Or better still, I could run you back to Wildfell and you could collect your bike some other time."

Janet hesitated, but something made her reject the offer of the lift.

"Just as you say," he agreed. "I'll see you on your way, at least as far as the top of the dale. I've an old boneshaker here that was bequeathed to me with the bungalow. Its former owner had apparently no further use for it, but I use it sometimes."

Janet protested that there was no need for him to go with her, but he insisted with a queer sort of doggedness that she could not turn aside.

"I'll see you safely into the dale," he repeated.

The path over the fell by Parson's Crag was a shorter way, cutting off the switchback windings of the dale road by over three miles, but it could not be argued that it was an easier way. It was time, however, that really mattered, and Janet pushed her bicycle up the steeper gradients with the hope in her heart that nothing had gone wrong at the farm while she had been away.

Mark would bring Jonathan home at seven, and she hoped to reach Wildfell before then.

"Janet," Tom said with a strange note of fatality in his pleasant voice, "you've got a lovely flat tire!"

"Oh, no!" She bit her lip in vexation. "Not a puncture at this stage!"

"We can only investigate and hope for the best," he answered phlegmatically.

"I pumped the tires up before I left."

"These things happen, I'm afraid." His mouth looked slightly grim as he glanced up at the hill in front of them. "There ought to be a beck flowing down here somewhere," he observed.

"Then you *do* think it's a puncture?"

"I guess so." She noticed his swift look at the lowering sky, but not the scarf of mist hanging on the hill above them. "I'm hoping it won't take long."

It took a quarter of an hour for them to trace the stream among the thick bracken and carry her bicycle to it, and by the time the puncture had been fixed they were shrouded in mist.

"We'll have to go back," Tom said. "It's the only way."

"We can't. *I* can't. We're more than halfway to Wildfell, and it may be quite clear on that side of the fell. You know what it can be like wispy and clear in patches."

"Yes," he agreed without a great deal of conviction, "it can be."

"We can follow the path," Janet said. "That's one thing."

Tom wheeled his bicycle upward in silence.

"I'm sorry, Tom," Janet apologized. "I didn't mean to pull you into anything like this."

"I came of my own accord," he reminded her. And I believe it was my idea that you come to tea in the first place. I also suggested that you go back this way."

"Because I was in a hurry and wouldn't leave the bike I'm more to blame than you are."

Half a mile farther on their voices sounded hollow against the wall of fog. Instead of decreasing it had intensified, and they could see little more than a yard ahead of them.

"It's a sea harr," Janet said uneasily. "It must stretch all the way in from the coast."

"You're going to get very wet and we're not going to be able to ride a yard!" he answered irritably.

He did not say that they should have turned back when he suggested it, and perhaps the retreat would scarcely have benefited them even if they had decided to make it. The mist swirled down behind them as thickly as it lay ahead and they were soon wet through.

There was no real danger, Janet assured herself; only the maddening delay as they pushed their bicycles up to the Crag.

Almost before they realized that they had come upon it, the giant, pinnacled outcrop of stone looming up out of the wavering mist.

"At least we've got this far," Janet said, repressing an involuntary shiver. "We'll soon be going downhill, and that will help."

"You're going to catch your death of cold," Tom observed contritely. "I should have known better than to come this way when I saw the sky."

"Was that what you were wondering about?" she asked. "I'm a poor daleswoman, Tom, forgetting my weather signs so easily."

"You've been away for a long time," he said. "Janet, have you come back for good?"

She hesitated, her lower lip held between her teeth in the manner she had when she had when she was unsure about an answer.

"I don't know. I think it will depend on Mark."

"On Mark?"

"I'm a necessary evil just now, Tom. Mark wouldn't have me at Wildfell if there was a suitable substitute. Ruth, for instance."

She thought that he drew back at the mention of Ruth's name, but the swirling fronds of mist were too thick around him for her to see his expression clearly. He remained silent for a long time before he replied, and she felt that he had withdrawn a confidence that he might have made in other circumstances.

"Mark has changed a lot," he said slowly. "I didn't have any personal contact with him over the sale of Scarton. It was all done through our lawyers. Mark made no bones about it being purely a business deal, and it might just as easily have been a deal between strangers."

Janet did not know what to say. These revelations only served to accentuate her own impression of change, doing nothing to explain the underlying reason for it.

"Something has hardened him," she said unsteadily. "He has grown so like his father that they might be one and the same person."

Tom plodded on a few steps ahead of her, silent and thoughtful, his dark bulk looking immense through the enveloping grayness. The mist was not lifting, and at the edge of the ridge it clamped down on them like some tangible thing.

"We'll have to sit this out," Tom decided. "I can't see a blessed thing!"

Janet felt exhausted. The uphill climb, pushing her bicycle, had tired her beyond belief, and her hair and skin were damp with mist.

"We'd better go back to the Crag," Tom advised. "It's higher, and it's the only comparative shelter for miles." He looked down at her, contrite in his apology. "It's the only solution, Janet, till this clears."

They made their laborious way back, leaving their bicycles on the ridge. The Crag was not exactly an effective shelter, but it broke up the wall of mist and they were able to squeeze themselves into a crevice in the rock and watch the swirling, wraithlike columns drifting past them.

It was over an hour before Tom thought that it might be clearing beyond the ridge.

"Shall we try again?" he asked.

Janet nodded automatically. She was stiff with cold by now and her lips seemed frozen so that speech was difficult. In her heart, too, was the thought of Mark, waiting at Wildfell. Would he be anxious by this time, or angry, or merely impatient at her folly?

Before they reached the ridge a sudden wind blew up and Tom drew a deep breath of relief.

"That should do it!" he exclaimed. "I thought we were marooned up here for the night!"

Their laughter still sounded hollow, echoing back from the surrounding crags, and then, suddenly, there was another sound. Mingling with the rising wind, it was like a distant drumbeat, and it was seconds before they recognized it.

"A horse!" Tom said.

The sound came nearer and Mark's name beat against Janet's mind to the accompaniment of dismay. Mark had come to look for her, yet it could not be out of any personal sense of concern.

Horse and rider drew close, and Tom hailed them.

Mark swung down from the saddle, striding toward them through the lifting haze. Janet saw his face, strained and anxious for a moment before he recognized Tom, and then it was as if he had seen a ghost. The mask of reserve and cynicism that he habitually imposed upon himself was torn away, and he stood staring at her companion as if he could not believe the evidence of his own eyes.

"Mark, I'm so sorry," Janet apologized quickly. "I'm sorry to have given you all this trouble. I went to Kirby Allerton this afternoon with the grocery order and met Tom...."

The look on his face silenced her. Mark did not want to hear her explanation. He was staring at Tom, the unleashed fury in his eyes terrible to see.

"Look here, Mark," Tom began, but he got no further. That look of Mark's had silenced him, too. Yet for a moment he seemed to be struggling with an almost overwhelming desire to retaliate, but Mark seemed to dwarf him. Tom dwindled before the other's fury as if he had been no more than a guilty schoolboy.

"You're on Langdon property here, Ransome," Mark reminded him in a voice of ice. "I'll thank you to keep on your own side of the fell."

"Mark!" Janet protested, but she knew that he did not hear her.

"All right, Janet, don't worry!" Tom said quietly. "I'll get back."

He did not say that they might meet again. He appeared to be accepting Mark's ultimatum meekly and without argument, which was as unlike the old Tom Ransome as the challenge itself was unlike the Mark she had once known and still loved.

Tom took up his bicycle from the side of the road where they had abandoned them an hour earlier.

"Leave that," Mark ordered when Janet attempted to do the same. "Heber can collect it in the morning."

Before she could protest he had lifted her and swung her into the saddle, vaulting up behind her without even as much as a glance in Tom's direction. She knew that he was angry, more bitterly angry than she had ever seen him in all her life before, and her own impatience seemed pointless.

"Good night, Tom," she called. "And—thank you!"

Mark stiffened. They were so close now that she could feel his heartbeats pounding out their fury.

"I could walk—quite easily," she protested in a stifled whisper. "There's no need for this, Mark. I'm not—hurt or anything."

"You're soaking wet and quite likely to catch a chill," he told her harshly. "What madness made you stay on the other side of the fell when you knew what the weather was like?"

"I must have been too long away from the dale to remember all the signs," she said unsteadily. "I didn't expect to be caught like this, and I didn't see any harm in going to Tom's bungalow for a cup of tea when he asked me."

Her spirit, which had been momentarily crushed by Mark's anger, had reasserted itself. She felt his whole body tauten at the mention of Tom, and he dug his heels into the mare's flanks and sent the patient animal down the ridge at a trot.

"Whatever you feel about Tom Ransome," he said stonily, "your friendship with him must cease while you remain at Wildfell."

The arbitrary demand took her completely by surprise, but it also goaded her to a new anger. She supposed that he could feel her trembling as she answered.

"I'm not exactly a child, Mark, and my choice of friendships must remain my own. Unless you can give me a more concrete reason than your own dislike of Tom, I don't think I am going to be able to obey you."

His swiftly indrawn breath might have been anything from surprise to barely suppressed fury.

"Tom Ransome can have no part in your friendship or anything else," he said, "while you remain under my roof."

She knew then that further argument would be useless. She felt defeated and weak and cold, and foolish tears welled and gathered in her heart. Was this all there would ever be between them, this ceaseless conflict of two people reaching out blindly for different things? What did Mark want from life now? Was it only power and the satisfaction of ultimate revenge? If that was so, it would warp his whole nature in time and she would be forced to stand aside and watch without being able to help.

The mare's pace quickened as they neared Wildfell and once or twice she stumbled on the rutted road. Janet found herself thrown back against Mark, and instantly his arm tightened around her. She was pressed to a hard, unresponsive body where the heart beat slowly and heavily without even a tremor at her nearness.

Suddenly unable to bear the close proximity any longer, she twisted in the saddle.

"Let me down here, Mark," she demanded. "I can walk the rest of the way."

He held her relentlessly.

"You wouldn't be able to walk a yard," he said. "You're completely exhausted."

Slow, difficult tears spilled from her eyes, and she turned her head away.

"You know everything," she said childishly. "And you think yourself invulnerable."

She imagined the smile that must have curved his lips at her words, bitter and cynical as his reply.

"Perhaps it is just as well to be invulnerable, Janet. A woman in one's life can be the very devil."

"This woman isn't in your life!" she flashed in hurt anger. "Or ever would wish to be. You're far too changed for that, Mark. Too much different from what you used to be, too self-reliant and — and ruthless to live with for long!"

She expected anger, but he only laughed.

"Aren't you forgetting that you returned of your own free will?" he pointed out. "You asked to come back to Wildfell, Janet."

"Before I knew that you were master here! Before I knew how changed everything would be!"

"I didn't think that you found us changed. You said the other day that Wildfell would never alter in a hundred years."

"I wasn't thinking about the farm," Janet cried, brushing away the tears that she hoped he would not see because they were proof of her weakness. "Places don't change very much. Only people."

"Would it surprise you if I told you that I found you changed?" he asked.

"No. Nothing about you would surprise me, Mark," she said. "Not now. I could never have imagined you ruthless and cruel. I could never have considered you grasping and unfair and willing to kick a man when he was down."

There was a small silence in which his capturing arm did not relax its hold.

"Yet you believe me all these things and more?" he mused. "The knowledge could be enlightening."

"If you cared enough! Oh, I know that's what you mean! I know it doesn't matter to you what people think about you," she accused, "or how hurtful you are to someone like—like Tom."

His arm relaxed so suddenly that she had to grasp the saddle to steady herself.

"We won't discuss Ransome," he said frigidly. "I have no desire to see him at Wildfell or at the Grange."

They had reached the farm and were clattering across the cobbles of the yard. Mark swung his long body down from the saddle, his face harsh and gray beneath its tan.

Whatever had come between him and Tom Ransome was far more serious than the transfer of Scarton Grange from one to the other, Janet realized. She knew it without being told, just as she knew that nothing Mark would ever do would change her love.

"You'd better go in and have a word with my mother," he advised. "She's been in a state about you ever since six o'clock. Then you can get a hot bath and go to bed. I told Heber to boil some water when I set out in search of you. I wasn't sure what I would find."

Would it have mattered to him, she wondered dismally, if he had found her injured up there on the moor instead of just drenched to the skin and coldly miserable?

Squaring her shoulders, she went into Harriet's sitting-room.

"I heard the mare coming back and Mark's voice," Harriet said, a look of relief flooding over her face when she opened the door. "You've no idea how difficult it is just to lie here waiting, Janet, when things go wrong. We imagined all sorts of accidents when you didn't get back by six o'clock."

"Was Mark home so early?" Janet asked, trying to steady her voice. "I'm so sorry I've caused all this commotion, Mother Harriet, but I didn't think about the mist coming down, and neither did Tom."

"Tom Ransome?" Harriet asked. "Is he back in the dale for good?"

"He has a small property on the far side of Parson's Crag." Janet found it difficult to talk about Tom. "I think he means to settle down there, keeping chickens and pigs."

Harriet nodded.

"It was a great pity he had to sell the Grange," she said. Whatever stood between Tom and Mark, his mother knew nothing about it. There was no resentment in her, no grasping desire to possess the Grange. She looked tired and worn out by these past few anxious hours, and Janet forgot about Tom and Mark and put her arm protectively around the thin shoulders.

"I'll see you into bed," she offered. "Have you had your supper?"

"Heber brought me some milk." Harriet glanced at the untouched glass on the table at her elbow. "I'll drink it up now that you're here safely." Suddenly the frail hands were clinging to Janet's strong ones. "I don't know what I would have done if anything had happened to you out there on the moor," Harriet said unsteadily. "I'm getting to be an old woman, Janet weak and afraid."

"You'll never be that!" Janet bent to kiss the sparse gray hair. People like me don't disappear so easily, even up here on the moor!"

"I suppose I've come to lean on you," Harriet acknowledged with a sigh. "It oughtn't to be that way, Janet. You should be free to go again, if you wish."

"Don't let's talk about that sort of thing just now," Janet said almost sharply. "I've only just come back."

The blue eyes smiled, and Harriet Langdon relaxed among her pillows.

"It's such a comfort," she breathed, "to know that you are here with Mark."

With Mark! Something crushed and broken in Janet laughed hollowly at the hope. By the morning Mark would have shut himself away again behind his barriers of reserve and coldness, without need of anyone.

"Go and change," Harriet advised. "You're wet through and shivering with cold. You'll get your death."

The kitchen was full of steam and a huge fire roared in the grate. Mark had lifted the wooden top off the big enamel bath that stood in the corner and dragged it to the hearth, where he was filling it with buckets of water from the copper.

"It's primitive," he remarked with a grim smile, "but it will answer your purpose. Don't stand about till you catch cold."

If she could have imagined kindness in his tone she might have collapsed ignominiously in front of him, but Mark could only be concerned about the possibility of having someone ill with pneumonia on his hands when there was outside work to be done.

She stumbled upstairs to find her dressing gown and a change of underwear, thinking how different things would be if only Mark would be kind.

"Janet," a thin voice called through the wall, "is that you?"

She went to Jonathan's bedroom door.

"Yes, darling! I've come back."

"I thought you had gone away for good."

The voice was sleepily distressed and two little arms were stretched out toward her in the half dark. She bent down and let them encircle her neck.

"Go to sleep, Jonny!" she whispered. "I'm here now."

The child's welcome, his need of her, made her heart swell as she descended the uncarpeted stairs, and she thought that Wildfell held some sort of warmth, after all.

The kitchen was deserted now, and she barred the outer door to the houseplace and took her bath with a strange, inexplicable feeling of well-being seeping through her for which she could not offer any reasonable explanation except that two people, at least, had welcomed her return.

CHAPTER THREE

As the days of that mild autumn slipped away and the moor changed through all the shades of russet and orange and purple that nature could devise, Janet scarcely realized how swiftly the last six years were   ng from her memory.

If she thought of her former life at all, she thought of it as a pleasant interlude belonging to the past. The white-sanded bay cleaving the blue water of the Mediterranean like a sickle had never been so real to her as these vast reaches of moorland rolling endlessly to the horizon or their meeting with the hills in the north. This was her country, the life to which she had been born, and only an old man's stubborn harshness had separated her from it for a time.

Had she been asked to contrast the two, she would not have been able to do so with any finality. Her six years of luxury in the south of France as Miss Pope's companion had taught her much, but most of all they had taught her to appreciate the simple things of life, the fundamental things.

If Mark had been fairer, if he could have thrust aside his sorrow and preoccupation with the past even for a moment, she might have found life perfect, but as it was he had withdrawn even more firmly into his shell after their emotional encounter on the moor and she felt that she could not reach him.

He seemed, in fact, to be avoiding her, if she could bring herself to believe that he took even such a small interest in her comings and goings.

Her visit to Kirby Allerton was not repeated for several weeks and then, as was almost inevitable in so small a place, she met Tom Ransome again.

"I was almost about to storm the citadel!" he greeted her lightly as he caught up with her on the main road. "I thought you must have changed your mind and gone away."

"We've been very busy," she explained with a slight tug at her heart, remembering the scene under Parson's Crag when Mark had thrown the full fury of his hatred in Tom's honest face. "We are having a bathroom put in at the farm."

"Was that Mark's idea or yours?" Tom asked, with lifted brows. "I thought Mark objected to improvements on principle."

"He made the offer," Janet said, "and I was grateful. Of course, it was really for Jonathan's benefit."

He gave her a quick, searching look, dismissing the subject of Mark to ask, "Dare I invite you to tea again? I have something I want to show you."

The thought of Mark, standing between them, was ever present. Janet knew that Tom acknowledged it with a certain amount of resentment, considering it unfair, as she had done.

"Why not?" she said. "There's plenty of time, and no mist!"

"To bring Mark in search of you?" There was a strange inflection in his voice, half bitterness, half regret. "Perhaps he has convinced you that our friendship is not to be desired?"

Janet flushed.

"That's absurd," she countered. "We have known each other all our lives."

He looked away from her candid eyes, his smile fading.

"That might have counted for something," he said. "Or no one would have believed."

"Between you and Mark?"

"Between all of us."

She could not understand, but she would not question him further. If she had made up her mind to defy Mark's authority, even subconsciously, she could not discuss him with the object of his displeasure.

Tom appeared to accept the fact, keeping their conversation on a light note as they walked toward the bungalow.

"Well," he demanded when they came within sight of the nearest field, "what do you think of them?"

Janet looked over the hedge at the new pigs with all a countrywoman's pleasure.

"They're Landrace, aren't they?" she asked. "You're aiming at the best, Tom."

"They represent a fortune, as far as I am concerned, and I stand or fall by them," he admitted. "I can't afford to lose out on this venture, Janet," he added more seriously. "It's a—sort of final throw."

She found herself wondering how that could be. Scarton Grange and all that land at the foot of the dale could not have changed hands for nothing, and Tom would have had to be heavily in debt to get through so much money in so short a time. He had never wanted for anything when his father was alive, but he had not been the spendthrift type who would go easily through a fortune afterward.

They took their tea before a roaring fire in the bungalow's sitting room. It was Mrs. Bowes's day off. She had gone to Darlington, Tom explained, to visit her sister.

"The best thing about a housekeeper is that she leaves you entirely free to please yourself on her days off," he laughed. "If you don't want to eat, you needn't. She doesn't fuss and believe you're going to die of starvation before she gets back in the evening!"

"Whereas a wife invariably does?" Janet smiled.

"I believe so."

Something in his tone made her turn to look at him. If it had been Mark, she would not have been surprised by the note of cynicism, but Tom was far too straightforward a person to hide his feelings behind a mask of sarcastic reserve.

"Have I surprised you?" he asked. "I didn't mean to. Forget what I said."

Janet couldn't dismiss things so easily. She felt, suddenly, that Tom needed her friendship.

"It didn't sound like you." she said. "I've always thought of you as the thoroughly domesticated type."

As soon as she had uttered the words she was sorry. Tom's face had contorted in a look of the most intense pain and his eyes fell away from her friendly regard, as if to hide the naked emotion that lay there, revealed in spite of himself.

"I'm sorry," Janet whispered. "I didn't mean to intrude."

He stooped to put an extra log on the fire, the fine contours of his expressive face flung into sharp relief against the leaping flames.

"The last time we met," he said, "I wondered how much you knew about me, Janet. About these six years you were away from the dale."

"I seem to be hopelessly ignorant," she told him. "I wrote to Mrs. Langdon, of course, but she hardly ever mentioned you. She was concerned about Ruth and Mark leaving the farm, but I don't think she had the heart to write much about that, either. Mr. Langdon took such a harsh view of everything, and she did a lot for the sake of peace. Now, when I look back, I realize that it must have been a great blow to him and a bitter disappointment when we all left the dale so quickly after one another."

"He could have consoled himself with the fact that he practically turned you out."

The bitterness and frustration in the remark was unmistakable, and he prodded the fire savagely as he waited for her to speak.

Janet did not know what to say. This was a new Tom, with a strange, leashed resentment burning in him and a bitter, unforgiving mouth.

"We can't fasten all the blame where it doesn't belong, Tom," she tried to say fairly. "At least, I can't. I wanted to go. I made my bed and I had to lie on it, as Matthew Langdon would have pointed out if only he had had the chance." She tried to smile. "In some ways he was right, you know. Right about me, I mean. I belonged in the dale, Tom. I should never have left it."

"None of us should have gone." He got to his feet with a violence unusual in him. "We should have stayed and faced it out. Why does youth have to make so many mistakes and go on regretting them for a lifetime afterward?" he demanded.

"Sometimes they can be put right." She was trying to offer him consolation, but she knew that it was too late. "Tom, isn't there some way for you, at least?"

He turned, looking down at her with a world of torment in his eyes.

"You know that I am married?" he said.

The blunt statement shocked her, its bleakness carrying tragedy.

"No," she said, "I didn't know."

He took a swift turn about the firelit room, coming back to stand beside his vacant chair, but he did not sit down in it. He stood leaning on one of the wings, staring into the fire.

"I married hastily, when I thought there was no hope for Ruth and me," he said. "I went to London and flung a lot of money around, just having a good time and trying to forget that I had ever been in love, back here in Comerdale. I had what my father called 'a spree,' and I ended up with a wife I didn't even know. It was a reckless thing to do, but I would have put my back into the job of making a go of it if things had been different." He paused and then rushed on, as if the telling of all this was essential to them both. "Don't think I'm whining about it or trying to shirk the blame, Janet. I'm not. I was as much responsible for the failure we made of everything as Lucia was in her own way. I wanted her to come back here to the dale, and she was an actress and wanted to go abroad. She had some sort of doubtful contract to fulfill in Singapore, and she was furious when I wouldn't go with her. Poor Lucia! She wanted success so much that she would have tried anything. I couldn't dissuade her. A month after we were married she set sail, and six weeks after that I heard that she was dead."

Janet's breath ran out in a small, surprised gasp. She had not expected this, and the pain in Tom's voice was enough to tell her that she had only heard part of his story.

"Three months later," he added in a strained undertone, "she turned up again, out of the blue. She really had been presumed killed in an ambush on her way into the interior to do some show or other. A body had been found and presumed to be hers, but Lucia had escaped. She had lived up-country for a month or two and then come back to civilization to find me." He straightened. "It all seems incredible, doesn't it? These things just don't happen in the ordinary way, but they happened to me."

"And your wife is still alive?" Janet asked.

"And still demanding money. At present, she is in Switzerland."

The brief finality of the statement sank into the lengthening silence between them. Tom stood where he was, without moving, like something turned to stone by the very intensity of his unhappiness, and Janet sat with her hands clasped tightly together, aware that the growing bond between them had been curiously strengthened by his revelations.

There was no need for Tom to tell her that he was in love with someone else. The truth was there on his face plainly to be seen. They had both given their love hopelessly.

"I wish I could help," she said at last. "It's all so wasteful a waste of so much loving."

He moved then, turning to look out through the window.

"There's nothing we can do, is there?" he said. "That's the damnable bit. I should never have burdened you with half a tale."

Not till long afterward was she to realize that she had heard only half of Tom Ransome's story.

"I don't feel burdened, Tom," she said, getting up and fastening her coat. "Only terribly sorry for you. I hope what you are doing here will be some compensation to you." She stood beside him at the window, looking out across the small paddock and the meager adjoining fields, contrasting them subconsciously with the lush acres of Scarton Grange. "Sometimes it's best to begin again," she added gently.

"I'm giving it a trial, anyway." He turned to her with a forced smile. "You'll come again, Janet?" he asked.

"If I'm in Allerton," she promised. "But you know how isolated the dale can be in winter. We're beginning to stock up with food already."

"Which means that you do intend to stay at Wildfell?"

In her heart she knew that she could not answer him with any truthfulness. A hundred conflicting emotions made a definite decision impossible.

"I don't know, Tom," she confessed. "I'll stay while I'm still needed, I suppose."

"While Mark needs you?"

"In an indirect way. There's Jonathan, you see, and Mrs. Langdon."

Tom pursed his lips.

"I never thought that Mark would turn like this," he said.

The words pursued Janet all the way back to Wildfell. It was not only in her own imagination that Mark was changed. Everybody noticed it.

He was standing with Jonathan at the paddock gate when she wheeled her bicycle across the yard.

"We've had a man here," Jonathan informed her without preliminary. "He had a great big car that wouldn't turn in the yard!"

Janet looked at Mark.

"A friend of yours," he supplied. "I sent him after you to Allerton."

"A friend of mine?"

"Of your happier days, I presumed. He seemed most concerned about you after he had looked around here. He left his card."

Jonathan had run into the house and came back with a small cardboard oblong in his hand.

"I've got it!" he cried. "The man left it on the dresser an' I reached it with a chair!"

Janet took the visiting card, her heart beating uncomfortably fast under Mark's coolly indifferent stare, and for a split second the name on it meant nothing to her.

Charles Grantley, she read, and then a flood of warm, excited color rushed into her cheeks. She was remembering all Charles Grantley's former kindness and the fact that they had been good friends for almost six years.

"I'm terribly disappointed at missing him," she said, looking up at Mark. "It's Miss Pope's nephew."

Mark unfastened the girth from the pony and slid Jonathan's saddle from its back.

"So you did miss him?" he observed. "It seemed strange in a place as small as Kirby Allerton."

The color receded from Janet's cheeks as quickly as it had come, leaving her pale and tense as she faced him.

"I met Tom Ransome in the main street," she said. "There was something he wanted me to see at the bungalow and I saw no real reason why I shouldn't go there. I stayed for tea."

Her words were more keenly edged than she had meant them to be, and her tone had sounded defiant. Mark did not speak. Instead, he handed over the saddle to Jonathan, striding off across the yard in the direction of the sheep pens, where Heber and the cowman were working on a fence, his mouth grim, his whole attitude one of contemptuous dismissal.

Left alone with Jonathan, Janet stared down at Charles Grantley's visiting card with the tears stinging at the back of her eyes.

"Will the man in the car come back?" Jonathan asked

eagerly. "He gave me a ride to the end of the cart track!"

"Did you like him, Jonny?"

He paused, bewildered by the question.

"Yes," he said after a moment's consideration. "As much as Heber."

Janet smiled, because Heber and the cowman made up Jonathan's entire male world, apart from Mark, and she knew that Mark stood in a class apart where his son was concerned. Jonathan worshipped him, whatever anyone else might think about him.

When the child was in bed and Mark came in, throwing his heavy riding boots aside, she asked if Charles Grantley had left any message for her.

"He expected to pick you up in Allerton," he said, crossing to the kitchen to wash his hands at the sink. "No doubt he felt that a meal in a civilized atmosphere would do you a lot of good. He was going on to Middlesbrough, I believe."

"He has something to do with steel," Janet said, ignoring his taunt about the change of atmosphere. "I would have liked to see him again. We have known each other for almost six years."

"So he informed me." He turned to dry his hands on the towel behind the kitchen door. "He also seemed to consider that your mutual attachment did not lie wholly in the past. He hopes to see you again."

"Charles was always generous and so completely understanding," she said, wondering immediately why she hoped to pierce Mark's indifference with such an observation. "He was never unpredictable."

"An admirable quality in a man," he agreed dryly. "Perhaps you mean to marry him, Janet?"

Her face flamed scarlet at the taunt.

"I couldn't do better!" she assured him. "Charles would make an excellent husband."

"With so much to offer, I couldn't but agree." His words and tone were deliberately cruel, although she could not see his face very clearly in the dim half-light of the low-ceilinged room.

"That wouldn't be my reason for marrying him," she felt goaded to answer. "Material things don't count as much as you think, Mark, when it comes to one's life's happiness."

He moved, coming a pace or two toward her. In the uncertain light his eyes glittered scathingly.

"Do you really believe that, Janet?" he said. "If so, you have certainly changed."

There was no kindness in his voice, no hint of forgiveness. She could not beg him to believe that she had always wanted love his love and had only made a hideous mistake in not recognizing the fact earlier. Mark himself was far too changed for that. He was a stranger, a hard, unbending man, to whom forgiveness was synonymous with weakness and lack of personal pride.

"You'll never understand," she said, "because you'll never want to!"

He stood behind her, very close.

"I have disciplined myself to restrict my wants, Janet," he said. "In that direction, at any rate. I have been in love deeply in love and once is enough for me."

The atmosphere was tense with the force of his emotion and the strength of the passion that had moved him to make such an admission. Janet felt that she dared not move, in case she should be consumed by it. She could not turn to see the confession of his love for someone else burning in Mark's eyes, Mark who had once been hers

He had forgotten that love now, dismissing it as a puny, childish affair in the face of the mature adult passion that now held him and of which Jonathan was the

concrete proof. He had loved and suffered and lost, and
that had made him the man he was, the kind of man he
would always be.

She felt small and defeated and forlorn, yet he expected
her to carry the burden of their living at Wildfell without
complaint and without reference to the past. When he
walked away she stood quite still where he had left her,
almost as if she could not move.

Goaded by his coldness and the ruthlessness in him
that continued to exclude her, she faced the future with a
hopelessness that she had never known before. Even
when loyalty to Miss Pope had kept her in the Riviera
sunshine, there had always been the thought of Mark and
the hope of returning to his love, but now that was gone.
He had shown her so plainly that he had no need for her
apart from helping his mother and Jonathan.

Sitting beside Harriet in the long winter evenings while
Mark worked at his books in the distant business room,
she might come to accept the limitations of such a life, but
just now her heart cried out for the warmth of belonging
and the love that had once been hers.

Slowly she turned and went to her own room, flinging
herself face downward on her bed, but the tears that she
expected did not flow. A hard band of pain pressed
against her temples and her heart felt as if it must burst.
Why did life have to be like this? Why did love have to be
so cruel?

She thought that she could not stay at Wildfell another
day.

I've tried to tell Mark, she thought. *I've got to go away.
I can't stay and go on loving him like this!*

She turned, staring at the ceiling, listening to Jonathan
murmuring in his sleep in the room next door. He had
been excited by his busy day, by the completion of the new

bathroom with its running water and the visit of the man in the car who had given him a ride to the end of the cart track

Perhaps Charles Grantley was the solution to her problem, Janet thought dismally. If she married Charles, Mark would go out of her life forever.

But not his memory. Memory had a way of holding on, securing you by its silver threads. You could not break them or tear them ruthlessly away, because the fragments clung.

There was Harriet, too. Harriet and Jonathan were the ties that would bind her to the dale in spite of everything, in spite of heartache and coldness and tears. Harriet was so frail now that any sudden shock or disappointment might break her completely, severing the last weak strand that held her to life.

And Jonathan? The child had twined small, eager fingers about her heart, and she knew that she loved him as if he had been her own son.

Mark, wrapped up in his sorrow and hardened by his experience during those lost years when he had left Wildfell, could not take these other loves away from her

CHAPTER FOUR

CHARLES GRANTLEY reappeared at Wildfell two days later.

Janet saw the car coming over the ridge of the fell and down the dale road from Kirby Allerton, her heart beginning to beat wildly as she wondered what Mark would think. She had a right to a visitor, however, and Mark had expected Charles to come back.

When the car drew up, Mark was nowhere to be seen, although he had been working in the near fields all morning.

"Charles!" she cried, gripping her visitor's hand. "I wondered if you would come back."

"You didn't expect me to be right on your doorstep and not come?" he asked, holding her hand with the proprietorial air of a man who is determined not to be turned down a second time. "It's nearly two months since I put you into that train at King's Cross, and you said you would write when you got the time!"

He looked about him, as if he had little doubt why she had not written, and Janet felt confused and rather angry at his silent criticism. This primitive way of life would appall Charles; he would not be able to find anything of beauty in these stark moors and the distant, shadowy hills that she looked upon as home.

"We've been so busy with the harvest," she excused herself, "but I really meant to write. In a place like this, Charles, the days just slip past. There's so much to do."

He looked down at her hands with their closely filed fingernails and the little scars on them where Wildfell had left its mark.

"Apparently," he observed dryly. "How long do you intend to stay?"

She looked away from the swift demand in his gray eyes to the distant tips of the pines above the Grange.

"I belong here, Charles," she said. "I think I've made up my mind about that."

"But it's nonsense!" he protested. "You've your own life to lead."

"Perhaps this *is* my life," she said

He raised querulous eyebrows

"Married to a hill farmer?"

"Not married to anyone."

"Dare I repeat myself to remark that that is more nonsensical than ever?"

"Why should it be? It is what I have decided."

"Look here!" He took her by the shoulders, turning her to face him. "We've got to talk this over seriously, Janet. Quite seriously this time. I thought you had come back here because you were interested in this Langdon fellow, but as it's not the case, then he will have to find someone else to do his household chores for him. You told me once that you left to escape this sort of thing. Why should you come back to it now?"

"Perhaps because I am older and a little wiser."

"And because you consider it your duty to the old lady? But Langdon isn't penniless. He made quite a point of showing me the remainder of his property, the land he calls the Grange."

"I couldn't ask Mark to pay me for what I am doing, or to get anyone else," Janet said.

"So it is a labor of love?" He laughed abruptly. "Janet, you are still hopelessly transparent, I'm afraid!"

"Don't laugh at me, Charles," she appealed. "Why did you really come?"

"To convince you that there was no escape from marrying me in the end!" He released her hand and turned back toward the car. "I'm not going to pretend that I have succeeded, but then I haven't exactly failed, either, have I?"

He slid in behind the steering wheel and his glance suddenly shot up and held hers, drawing out all the uncertainty and indecision that had lain in her heart for weeks.

"Don't bother to give me your answer now," he advised. "I can wait for it, since I've already waited the best part of six years. We've known each other for a long time, Janet. The future would be worth a second thought   our future together."

She tried to protest, but he had started the engine and let in his clutch to drive away.

"Won't you stay for something to eat?" she asked, remembering that he had not met Harriet. "Mrs. Langdon will think it bad-mannered for me not to have asked you."

"And what will your farmer think?" he asked, laughing softly. "No, Janet, I've a feeling that I'm not going to be entirely welcome in Mark Langdon's stronghold, but when he's crushed your spirit completely I'll be waiting to pick up the pieces and stick them together again."

She longed to say that it was he who was talking nonsense now, but the truth of what he had said was like the growth of a strange seed that had been lying dormant in her own mind ever since her return. Mark's coldness seemed to have a strange purpose, and if it was to chastise her for the past he was surely succeeding.

Unhappily, she watched Charles drive away.

"I may see you in London before long," he called back to her through the open window. "You'll be getting a letter from Aunt Emily's lawyers that will explain everything."

"Have we had a visitor?" Harriet asked when Janet carried the tea tray into the sitting room half an hour later. "I thought I heard a strange voice."

"Yes," Janet admitted half-guiltily. "I should have brought him in, Mother Harriet, but he didn't want to stay. It was Charles Grantley, Miss Pope's nephew."

"The one who inherits most of her money?" Harriet asked. "You told me about him. I would have liked to meet him."

"He was on his way back to London." Janet looked preoccupied. "I'm sorry Jonathan missed the car. He thought it something quite out of this world when he saw it on Tuesday!"

"He told me about it," Harriet smiled. "Mechanical things are all he thinks about tractors and cars and the like. I wonder if he's going to be a good farmer, as Mark wants."

"Isn't it early to say?" Janet moved to the window, wondering if Mark would come home to share their meal. "I suppose it's dangerous to place all one's ambitions for the future in a child. Mark demands so much of Jonathan even now."

"Mark was always something of an idealist, deep down," Harriet mused. "He put a store on some things that other men would never give a thought to. He was gentle and kind as a boy."

Harriet's defense of her son was infinitely pathetic. Although she could not explain Mark's conduct even to herself, she believed that there must be a reason, somewhere, for the change in him. Her mother love had tried to probe beneath the surface and had failed, but she would not lose faith in him.

"It couldn't all be canceled out by one tragic mistake," Janet said unevenly. "It wouldn't be fair."

"Life is often unfair," Harriet said. "Tragedy and joy are sometimes ill-divided." She looked around her at the room that Mark had made the most comfortable one in the house. "Are you happy, Janet?" she asked abruptly. "I wish I could think that Mark and you would be happy."

"I'm happy to be with you," Janet said, turning from the window. "I'm glad to be home again."

It was true. Beyond all the pain and regret and loss there was a comfort and security in her homecoming that she could not explain. It had completed something that had been missing in her life. It had given her roots again.

"Bear with Mark," Harriet said unexpectedly. "He will come to need you."

If she did not believe that Mark would ever need her for himself, Janet could not tell Harriet so. The quality of fragility that she had noticed from the moment of her return was more apparent in Harriet now than ever. She seemed to be fading slowly before their eyes.

When she approached Mark about getting medical advice, he nodded and said that he would see to it at once. Yet when the doctor came from Kirby Allerton the following day, he said that there was very little change in Harriet's condition.

"She's getting old and her heart has been affected by the stroke she's had, of course, but with care and attention she should last for a long time yet," he declared.

He was a bluff, kindhearted man who had practiced among the fells for thirty years, and he considered Mark and Janet his children. He had brought them both into the world, and when Janet's mother had died six months after being widowed by the death of her husband at sea, it had been Dr. Gawthorne who had advised Matthew Langdon and his wife to adopt the child. He had believed then that Harriet would not have another child of her own, and he had known her desire for a daughter. When Ruth had been born a year later, he had scratched his head over the miracle, admitting the limitations of his knowledge with the heartiness of a man who could never be surprised at anything.

"It shows you," he had said, "that we don't know everything. Even in the twentieth century!"

Janet felt that Mark's fears about his mother had been put to rest, but there was an uneasiness in her own heart that was difficult to explain.

They were, at that time, beginning to prepare for the winter. Mark and Heber were busy out on the far reaches of the moor, repairing folds and building up the gaps in the dry stone dikes that marched over the hills in long, undulating gray lines. They were away all day, from sunrise to sundown, but even when he returned looking physically exhausted Mark would not give himself any respite. There was paperwork to do and the threshing to start at the Grange.

"If you want the car," he said at the end of the week, "to go to Allerton or Pickering, Heber will take you."

Janet thought that he might have offered to take her to Pickering himself, or even to York, where he had gone twice in the past few weeks to the Thursday cattle market, but it seemed that he had no intention of thrusting his company upon her.

"It will do if we can go to Allerton," she said. "Jonathan needs his hair cut, and I ought to have something done about my own."

He glanced at her briefly, as if he had noticed her personal appearance for the first time.

"Why don't you leave it as it is?" he said. "It suits you that way."

Her heart leaped foolishly at what might have been a compliment, or only Mark's way of telling her that nothing she could do about her personal appearance could ever influence him to notice her as a woman again.

"It's the way I wore it years ago," she said breathlessly, remembering how he had teased her in those far-off days about her ponytail, tied by a red ribbon. "It's too long to be fashionable."

He turned away, his hands thrust deep into his breeches pockets, his eyes remote.

"Get Jonathan's cut, anyway," he said. "Heber can take the afternoon off to drive you there and back."

Jonathan was always excited about a trip to Kirby Allerton, although he was not so sure about the suggested visit to the hairdresser.

"I don't want my hair cut off!" he protested vigorously. "It's getting cold, and you don't do the sheep in the winter."

"Sheep are different," Janet assured him firmly. "Their wool isn't exactly the same as yours! Besides, it's only little girls who have hair down to their shoulders, and you don't want them to put you in the wrong class when you go to school, do you?"

Jonathan looked suspicious.

"When am I going to school?" he demanded as they climbed into the car behind Heber.

"When you are five."

Mark had never made any reference to Jonathan's schooling or, for that matter, to his future at all. She did not know what he intended to do about the child's education or whether she would become dispensable if he sent Jonathan away. The school at Kirby Allerton would mean a journey of twenty miles a day, there and back, and there and back again, which would not present such an obstacle if she learned to drive the car.

Swift thoughts, tumbling into the future, as if she belonged there by Mark's side!

She thrust them from her to think of the present. There were extra stores to order, because it was always wise to lay in a stock of canned and boxed goods before the end of November. In that way any siege on the part of the weather would not find them unprepared. Smoked hams hung from the rafters in the house place and there were bins of oatmeal and other cereals in the dairy, ready for use. These were Mark's concern, and Heber's, but the stocking of the pantry shelves was the job of the woman of the house.

Janet had made her list, checking it over with Harriet before she left, and she left Heber to collect the parcels and stack them in the car while she hurried a reluctant Jonathan along the road to the hairdresser's.

Kirby Allerton was a typical daleland community nestling in a fold in the hills, with one main street, a war memorial, and an old Norman church surrounded by a moss-covered wall. The houses were all built of local sandstone and were nearly all alike, only the treatment of their tiny pocket-sized front gardens varying according to their owners' tastes. Half a dozen shops were scattered here and there among the dwellings: a hardware store, the post office, a grocery store, and three general dealers who kept everything from shoes to soap. Their window displays were unimaginative. Some of them bore the accumulated dust of years and were faded by the sun beyond recognition, but Jonathan never tired of gazing at them.

The hairdressing salon was behind the post office. It was kept by a Miss Sowerby, who had cut hair in the same way for the past thirty years.

Jonathan sat with his face screwed up and his eyes closed, twitching his nose every time Miss Sowerby's scissors snipped some hair away. He looked so comical that Janet wanted to laugh, but she dared not. That would have been the end of the haircutting.

"Now," Miss Sowerby exclaimed when her task was completed, "don't you look much better?"

Jonathan surveyed the shorn version of himself in the mirror facing him.

"I liked it better on," he said.

"Well, it's too late now!" Miss Sowerby commented breezily. "Are you going to sit in this nice chair and wait for auntie to have hers done?"

Jonathan looked at Janet. It was the first time he had heard her referred to as his aunt.

"I'll wait outside," he said after a pause.

Janet sat down in the chair before the mirror.

"He's growing fast, that little lad," Miss Sowerby commented, tying a clean apron under her customers chin. "I well remember Mark Langdon bringing him to the dale. Nobody knew anything about Mark being wed, and there was a nice bit of gossip at the time about him coming back with an infant to keep. You know what some folks up here are like. They want to know the far end of everything, and if they're kept in the dark they invent something worthwhile! There were some who said he had married unwisely," she ran on, "and others who declared he wasn't wed at all. Not legally wed, that is. I never passed an opinion myself, because he took full responsibility for the boy and even had him christened in the parish church. It was done by the vicar one Sunday morning not long after Mark returned to Wildfell, and he stood up in full view of the congregation and made himself responsible for the child. The boy was given his name the proud Langdon name but that was all anyone could find out. The vicar knew the whole story, of course, but he's not the man who would talk and break a confidence."

Janet had listened in frozen silence to this explanation of Mark's past, but Miss Sowerby was as much accustomed to the uncommunicative type of customer as she was to the more garrulous kind.

"I always say that people know their own affairs best," she decided. "Mark Langdon did what he thought right to do. You could never say that he was a dishonest lad or would let anyone down, although they tell me he's unsociable and keeps to himself now that he has come back from London and bought up half of Comerdale to add to Wildfell."

She paused, waiting for Janet to add her quota to the general news, but Janet sat silently staring into the mirror. She was picturing Mark standing in the village church with Jonathan in his arms, facing all those people he knew must be wondering about him and the years he had spent away from the dale, facing them silently while he accepted complete responsibility for the child he had brought back with him.

"Are you going to have it cut short?" Miss Sowerby asked, her head on one side as she surveyed her customer's hair through the mirror. "Your hair," she added when it did not seem that Janet understood. "Will you have it shorter?"

"No, No, just leave it as it is, with a little bit of a trim."

Janet's voice had sounded constricted and her thoughts were far away. All she wanted was to get out of Miss Sowerby's overheated little salon and into the open air.

A thousand conflicting emotions were stirring in her

heart, and her first instinct was to be alone. What she had just heard was not really new to her, but it hurt her to realize that Mark was still the subject of idle gossip on this side of the fell, at least. He was an enigma to these people, and he had proved himself silent and withdrawn, disdaining their opinion, so that gossip was kept alive almost inevitably. Mark had closed a door in their faces and they were consumed by curiosity to know what lay behind it.

It was the same door that had been shut against herself, Janet reflected, a door barred even to Harriet, because he didn't want them to see into the past.

She paid her bill, counting out the silver and leaving a tip that Miss Sowerby accepted with a grave air of putting it aside for her assistant. They walked to the door together and Miss Sowerby opened it. Almost immediately they were greeted by a wail of dismay coming from farther up the road.

"It's Jonathan!" Janet exclaimed, rushing out to find her charge being picked up by a stout little woman in blue tweeds.

"There now!" Mrs. Bowes was saying as she dusted him off. "Look at the hole you've made in the main street! There's nothing broken and you're not really hurt!"

Janet gave Tom Ransome's housekeeper a grateful smile.

"Thanks so much," she said. "I think he's just shaken a little."

"My knee's bleeding!" Jonathan pointed out with restrained dignity. 'I tripped an' fell," he added accusingly when it appeared that Janet was not so concerned about the accident as she might have been.

"So I see," she said. "There is some blood, but we can wipe it off with my handkerchief."

"It needs to be bathed," he declared. "There's gravel in it."

"There's always that risk," Mrs. Bowes acknowledged, turning to Janet. "Would you like to bring him along to the bungalow and get some disinfectant? It's just a step."

Janet looked around for Heber, but he was nowhere to be seen. The car, she supposed, would be parked in the yard of the Black Bull.

"We're giving you a lot of trouble," she said, but already Jonathan was stalking off toward the bungalow and they followed in his wake.

"Hello!" Tom said when he met them at the gate. "What's been going on here? Have you been in a private war of your own, Jonathan?"

"I fell in the road." Jonathan surveyed the knee, which had ceased to bleed. "It's got better just with coming here," he announced.

"You might have known that!" Tom laughed, hoisting him onto his shoulder. "We'll take a look at it, though, in case there is some dirt, and then we'll go and see the chickens, eh?"

Jonathan clasped his small hands under Tom's chin to steady himself on his precarious perch, laughing down into Tom's upturned face.

"Mr. Ransome's the best man I know with children," Mrs. Bowes remarked as Janet followed up the path to the bungalow. "It's a great pity he hasn't one of his own." Her mouth was suddenly compressed. "It doesn't seem likely he'll ever have one, either," she added, "with that wife of his gadding about the world as she does!"

Janet's gaze was fixed on the man and the delighted child riding his shoulders as if they had known each other for more than merely a few brief weeks.

"Yes," she said, "it's a great pity, Mrs. Bowes."

"The situation could change, of course," Dora Bowes observed. "I'd be willing to give up my job tomorrow if it meant that Mr. Ransome was going to be happier and have a real home."

They had reached the back door, where Tom had settled Jonathan on the kitchen table and was reaching down a bowl and a bottle of disinfectant from the shelf above the sink.

"You do it," Jonathan said when Janet came in, but he held on to Tom's hand.

"There, it's not so bad!" Janet announced five minutes later, sealing her handiwork with a sufficiently large elastic bandage. "But it looks imposing!"

They went to see Tom's chickens and the pigs, and inevitably they stayed for tea. It was after five o'clock before they left to find Heber grumbling at the front door of the Bull, although he had obviously just emerged from the landlord's back parlor. The landlord of the Bull and Heber were distantly related on their mothers' side.

"T'maister'll be fair flayed wi' anger at being kept waitin'!" he announced darkly. "Three hours to get a haircut, an' him wi' all the wark ti do!"

Janet was quite sure that the length of time they had spent in Kirby Allerton had not troubled Heber while he had remained in the Bull, but now she was troubled by it herself. Would Mark be anxious when they had not returned by dusk?

"You can drive quickly, Heber," she said. "We're not really very late."

"Ay, but it be dark an' there be still wark ti do!" Heber protested, grumbling his way in behind the wheel. "A flaysome business this hairdressin' nowadays!" he observed sourly. "Afore, ye could get it cut wi' a bowl, but noo it must be 'thinned' an' 'singed', as if t'lad were a turkey cock i'stead o' a normal human being!"

From long experience Janet knew that it was best to

pay no attention to Heber in his present mood. It did him good to grumble his way out of it, and he was almost his old self by the time they reached Wildfell

Mark was standing in the yard waiting for them. He had been at the paddock gates when the car's headlights had slanted over the hill, but he had walked back toward the house when it was obvious that no harm had befallen them.

"I've seen some chickens," Jonathan announced as Mark lifted him down from the front seat. "Lots an' lots of white ones, like the sea gulls in the winter, an' black ones, too, in another field. As black as crows!"

Janet's heart gave an uneasy jerk. For the first time she was remembering Mark's ban, but she had gone to Tom's bungalow in the most natural way in an emergency.

"I'm sorry we're late, Mark," she apologized. "But Jonathan hurt his leg and we went to Tom Ransome's to have it bathed."

If she had confessed that they had gone to a meeting of devils, the effect on Mark could not have been more terrible. His eyes blazed as they met hers across Jonathan's shorn head and his face was completely devoid of color as he demanded, "You took the child there?" His voice was as incisive and cutting as cold steel. "You must have known that it was against my will."

"I suppose I knew that, in a way." Her own voice was little more than a whisper. "But I didn't consider it at the time, Mark. It seemed the natural thing to do when Jonathan had been hurt."

He turned on his heel and left her. There was nothing more to be said in front of Heber and the child.

Shaken and upset by the encounter, Janet made her way to Harriet's room, drawing in a deep breath in an effort to compose herself before she opened the door.

"I'm thankful to see you back," Harriet greeted her. Mark has been pacing up and down out there at the paddock gate like a caged tiger for the past hour, wondering what could have happened to you."

Janet bit her lip.

"I know he must have been anxious about Jonathan," she said.

Harriet gave her an odd, searching look.

"Ay," she said, "maybe that. He guards the boy like a pearl above price. It doesn't always do, either. When you make an idol of something, or a fetish, there are often ways that bring you low."

"I don't think Mark spoils Jonathan so much now," Janet said. "Sometimes," she added slowly, "I think he is rather hard on him."

"That's because Mark has been hurt himself," Harriet said quietly. "Because he believes he has been too soft in the past. Soft and vulnerable. A man like Mark doesn't like to think that he can be caught twice by the same set of circumstances, and so he will go to the other extreme, in case there is a danger of it. Mark's not really hard. He's only determined that Jonathan won't be bruised by life. It's as if he had put on a sort of armor, Janet, and we can't reach him through it."

"I've tried," Janet said, "but it isn't any use, Mother Harriet."

It was a half-strangled confession of her love, and Harriet Langdon sighed heavily as she heard it.

"It isn't easy for two people like you and me to stand aside, Janet, and not try to help," she said. "It's not in our natures to turn a deaf ear or a blind eye to other people's sufferings, and so we'll always be hurt, right to the end. I used to think that I had Mark's confidence in most things, but since he came back from London there's been a blank wall between us that I can't see over or around or through. It would almost seem as if he was trying to hide something from me, something it would be far better that I should know."

"Mark wouldn't want to worry you with his troubles," Janet said. "He'd cope with a—difficulty alone rather than share it, I think. He was always like that. Always independent."

"Ay, that's so," Harriet agreed, but she was far from being satisfied.

Janet made her comfortable for the night and put Jonathan to bed when the new haircut had been sufficiently admired.

"I won't look like a girl now when I go to school, will I?" he demanded when Janet thought he was almost asleep.

"Of course not!" she comforted him. "I don't think you ever could, Jonny!"

He turned his head on the pillow, sublimely content, and a second or two later she tiptoed from the room, leaving him asleep.

The house was dark and quiet, but tonight it held an almost poignant friendliness. Every nook and cranny were so full of memories of her childhood, so well-remembered that she did not need the lamp she held to see her way. The gray panel of the window on the staircase gave light enough, and impulsively she turned down the wick and left the lamp burning low on the table on the upper landing. All the hardship she had known at Wildfell in the past and some of the frustrations of the last few weeks fell away from her, leaving her with only a feeling of deep and lasting satisfaction. The knowledge that life was not composed of the easier things had seeped gradually into her heart, yet this was something more. It was a fulfillment, a joy, a completion of her being that stretched out eagerly to the uncertain days of the future.

It was as difficult to question as it was to understand, but she could not push it from her with any real sense of decision. In it she found a vague, nameless comfort, which she hugged to herself jealously until she encountered Mark.

Immediately after their return from Kirby Allerton he had gone out with Heber, driving toward the Grange at what seemed a reckless speed even on the deserted dale road. She had heard the car returning three hours later, but Mark had not come in. Whether it had been Heber or Mark who had driven back she could not tell. The sound of the car's engine had rent the silence of the night for a moment, only to settle in more completely when the minutes ticked away and there was no movement within the house.

She put her darning basket away and looked at the clock. It was five minutes to twelve. Mark's supper still lay untouched on the table she had pulled toward the fire, a small gesture to his comfort that he would no doubt scorn when he saw it. She tried to think of Mark as cynical, but the events of the past few weeks were difficult to ignore. And now it seemed that he was remaining away because his anger was almost beyond control, because she had run contrary to his wishes and taken Jonathan to Tom Ransome's bungalow. The Mark she had known all these years ago would not have been so silent in his anger, but there would not have been the aloofness, the cold contempt that she felt she had now to contend with.

Restlessly she moved to the window where the yard beyond the undrawn curtains lay deserted in the faint glimmer of silver cast by a new moon. It stood above the hills, a thin sickle of light cut in the heavens like a scar, and she saw it for the first time without beauty, coldly withdrawn in a dark world of its own.

A movement in the room behind her told her that Mark was there.

How he had come in she did not know, but the fact of his sudden nearness sent her pulses racing and touched a bright, high color into her cheeks.

"There was no need for you to wait up."

There was nothing of churlishness in his voice; only a cold dismissal. Janet turned slowly to where he stood.

"It's my job to see that your supper is on the table when you come in," she said in a dead voice as she moved toward the oven. "I had no idea how long you would be."

The mounting tension between them had grown in his absence until it stood out like some tangible thing. Mark's face was hard, the look of his set mouth uncompromising.

"The times of my meals are a minor detail, Janet, as far as I am concerned," he said. "I must ask you to consider my wishes in other respects, however."

"You mean about taking Jonathan to Tom Ransome's?" she asked. "I've explained about that, Mark. It was unavoidable."

"These unavoidable events have a way of accumulating," he returned frigidly. "I would appreciate it if you would not take Jonathan to Kirby Allerton again."

"But that's unfair!" she cried passionately. "It's penalizing Jon for my mistake."

"Evidently you make mistakes easily and deliberately." His harshness was more apparent now, but somehow it was easier to meet than that first frigid contempt. "Jonathan understands that when I say a thing I mean it. He will not expect to go to Kirby Allerton again unless he is with me."

Disappointment swamped Janet for a moment, disappointment for herself and for Jonathan, because she knew how much he had enjoyed his afternoon's outing and the visit to Tom's bungalow. She saw him, suddenly, as a rather lonely little boy overshadowed by the dark shoulders of the dale and too much adult company.

"You are like your father, Mark," she accused sharply. "You will never let kindness or pity sway you too far."

He looked at her as if he was about to say something very much to the point, and then he crossed abruptly to the fire, staring down into its red heart as if he had remembered a vow of silence just in time.

"That may be," he said, "but the fact remains that my decision must stand. Jonathan must find other things to do here at Wildfell without going to Kirby Allerton to be amused by Tom Ransome."

"Tom has a way with children," Janet said heatedly, "which you might not understand. Jonathan likes him and he loved being at the bungalow. It was a—a sort of adventure for him. It was something quite new."

"Jonathan has no need to look for fresh worlds to conquer," he returned briefly. "He has Wildfell and Scarton Grange. Enough to be content with."

"He needs other children's companionship," Janet reminded him firmly. "There's no one here in the dale of his own age, and until he goes to school he's bound to be lonely. Children need one another. They need to see—another side of life as much as we do, Mark. Their minds have to be broadened, even at an early age. We can't force them into a mold of our making. Not because of—resentment and personal hurt, anyway. They've got to be free to be happy, at least."

"Jonathan is perfectly free to do as he wishes here in the

dale," he returned with finality. "So long as he realizes that those wishes can't run contrary to mine."

Janet felt defeated, but something lost yet defiant in her urged her to say, "You're being almost tyrannical about this, Mark. What would your wife think about her son's isolation, if she knew?"

The words had escaped her before she was even conscious of their forming in her mind. They had come straight from her heart, and their effect on Mark was something she never hoped to see again.

He stood back as if she had struck him, his face ashen in its sudden pallor, his mouth twisted in the bitterest of lines. It was his eyes, however, that held her, and she looked into them with a horrified knowledge of trespass. In them she saw an agony that shook him with a force even he could not control.

If the revelation was momentary, it was also shattering in its utter intensity. She drew back, scorched and humiliated by it, waiting for Mark to speak.

"I have no wife," he said slowly and distinctly, at last.

It was the old hard Mark speaking, the Mark who had won control over his emotions just in time. He turned before she could answer him, leaving her there with his deliberate confusion echoing to the rafters.

It would echo in her ears for the rest of her life, Janet thought; echo and echo down through the years   Mark's explanation of the past and his answer to the future.

CHAPTER FIVE

Two days after her unfortunate visit to Tom Ransome's bungalow, Janet received a letter from London.

Mark brought it in. He had met the mailman before he reached the box at the gate and he carried it up to the house with a bundle of others, all addressed to himself.

"Your admirers are nothing if not persistent, Janet," he observed, tossing it onto the table before her where it was impossible not to recognize the bold, mannish handwriting on the envelope. "I wonder how long we will be able to keep you in Comerdale?"

Surprised by the personal nature of the remark, Janet looked up at him.

"For as long as you have need of me," she said slowly.

He crossed to the window, standing with his back toward her.

"I brought you here for a reason," he said, "but it wasn't because I needed you."

His voice had sounded thick, his words clipped, and they stabbed straight to her heart.

"I wish I knew why it was," she cried. "If it was to hurt me, Mark—to humble me—you have already done that, but it can't have given you all the satisfaction you imagined. That sort of thing never does. It's like revenge. It burns itself thrusting the other person into the fire. If it was for revenge, Mark, you could have done it in another way."

"By refusing to let you come at all?" He turned, his gaze coldly calculating as his eyes met hers. "I think not, Janet. In any case, I have a feeling that you would have come back to the dale without my permission, even if it were only to prove how right you were about going away."

"You think something is holding me?" she asked unsteadily. "Something beyond my desire to stay?"

"I think you might want to go, but you feel that you owe it to my mother to stay."

It was amazing how near to the truth a person could come, Janet thought, without stumbling on the real truth.

"That should be reason enough for my staying," she told him. "So long as your mother needs me, Mark, I won't desert her."

His eyes flickered to the letter on the table and back again to her flushed face. It was as if her statement half surprised him, and for the first time Janet noticed that her letter bore a foreign stamp. A French stamp. She knew that Mark was aware of the fact and the color heightened in her cheeks.

"Whatever you think about me," she challenged, "at least give me the credit for some measure of fidelity. Your mother is ill. I shall stay here to nurse her until—until she is better."

She would not face the possibility of Harriet's early death. Her distressing frailness could be overcome by attentive nursing and good, nourishing food, and already she was eating more and responding in other ways. The slight paralysis was still there, but it had not increased. When her heart was stronger she might even be able to walk again.

That was looking months ahead, of course. Perhaps even years. Janet wondered if Mark had taken the same long view of the situation.

He went out without enlightening her, and she realized how little anyone would ever know of Mark's inward thoughts, of the emotions and desires and despairs that must shake him as they shook other men. One woman might come near to it, the one woman in his life, the desired confidante. She, Janet, had been Mark's first love, but she had been too young in those days to realize such things, to probe the depths of companionship and need. Love had been little more than an exciting new experience, accepted without knowledge, claimed by her as a right simply because she had loved and would be loved in return. She had no real thought of giving and taking and understanding in those days. The utter joy, the pleasure, the easiness of love had left her bemused and unthinking, and Mark had been older than she was at that time. Older and wiser in so many ways.

She picked up the letter he had brought, recognizing Charles Grantley's handwriting as she slit the envelope. Charles must be back in France, she realized, back at the villa, perhaps, and wanting her with him.

Vividly she pictured the calm blue bay with its curve of gleaming white sand and the deep green pines silhouetted against a cloudless sky; she heard the song of the grass-hoppers on a still night when the wind had dropped and the Mediterranean lay like black grass under a yellow moon, and it tugged at her heartstrings a little because for six happy years she had known a measure of contentment there, if not the absolute joy of complete assurance.

Charles's letter was brief and to the point, written in his usual forthright style:

This isn't a love letter. I've almost despaired of get-ting any response from you in that direction, although I mean to try again. It's strictly a business communication, my dear Janet, so you must not tear it up or lay it aside unread.

My London lawyers wish to get in touch with you. They also handled my aunt's business affairs, so you will not be surprised to hear that it is in connection with her will. She was very fond of you, my dear, and the money she has left you I am to administer in conjunction with Mr. Hambleton, of Hambleton, Hambleton and Wriseley. Their offices are in Lincoln's Inn, but I think it would be best if I took you there personally. I know you will feel saddened and perhaps confused by this business, so I think our early meeting is really necessary. I shall be in London in a week's time. Will you meet me there? There are also a few small matters in connection with my aunt's possessions that I think you can help to clear up. It would save me a great deal of searching among her personal belongings. Much as I loved her, I now realize that Aunt Emily was by far the most acquisitive woman I've ever known, and easily the untidiest! (I searched for hours for her birth certificate, only to come across it where the television license should have been!)

Will you send your reply to this to Kensington and I will pick it up at the apartment on my return?

Give my kindest regards to the hill farmer, but don't marry him.

It was signed "Yours devotedly, Charles", but underneath the lightness of its approach Janet could detect all Charles Grantley's sincerity and genuine wish to help her.

She was touched and grateful at the thought of the small legacy that her former employer had left her, and she thought that she might even ask Charles to let her have some little article belonging to his aunt as a keepsake. They had been a gay and happy trio on many an occasion during those six eventful years, and when the end had come she had been sorry, but that part of her life had never struck the strong roots that Wildfell had, reaching deep down into the secret places of her heart.

Perhaps she could marry Charles with a fair chance of being happy, but companionship and understanding were never a substitute for love. They had to go hand in hand with it. She knew that it was not in her to offer Charles second best, but she wrote back to him saying that she would do all she could to help him with his aunt's affairs.

It was most difficult to explain her journey to London to Mark, however.

"I'd like to be sure that your mother will be all right while I'm away," she said when she had explained about the letter. "It won't be for long. A couple of days will do."

"Will they?" he asked with some measure of doubt in his voice. "Isn't this really goodbye, Janet?"

"No," she said firmly. "I mean to come back."

He crammed tobacco into the bowl of his pipe with a savage gesture, but when he spoke his voice was quite cool.

"You're quite free to make your own decision in this," he assured her. "Martha Crosby is in circulation again, apparently, and would be willing to look in now and again."

"I don't think that's enough," Janet objected. "Martha does the rough work very well, but someone ought to be here with your mother all the time."

"I seem to have failed in that respect," he remarked almost casually. "Of course, the answer to my problem would be a wife."

The color ebbed slowly from Janet's cheeks.

"You're not offering me the position, are you?"

She hoped that her voice had been steady and as casually indifferent as his own. He was standing very near, regarding her with a peculiar intensity, although her back was turned towards him. She felt, somehow, that her slightest reaction would be known to him, and it made her uncomfortable.

"I did that once before," he answered slowly. "A man is a fool, Janet, who repeats himself too often."

She swung around to face him.

"You haven't a great deal of faith in love, have you?" she demanded in a stifled undertone. "But you'll come to need it, Mark. Someone's love will be necessary to you some day. You can't go on being   sufficient unto yourself forever. When you are older you will be alone at Wildfell." She cast a swift, almost despairing glance around the austere house place where they were standing. "And it will always be like this. You will have no comfort, nothing to make life full and easier for you."

Her voice dropped, shattering against the blank wall of his indifference, but she could not tear her eyes away from the expression on his face. She thought that he looked baffled for a moment and then incredulous, but almost as swiftly his eyes changed, darkening with some angry emotion that would not quite yield to derision.

When he spoke it was almost as casually as before, but he knocked out the contents of his pipe against the stone of the high mantelpiece as if it no longer held solace for him.

"What are you offering me, Janet?" he asked, coming back to stand beside her. "Companionship in my old age? A lukewarm passion when my blood has run thin?"

His nearness stifled any reply she might have made, any defense she might have put up. She was shaking from head to foot, and all she wanted was to escape. With an inarticulate little sound she sought to pass him, only to feel his hands like steel on her arms and her body crushed mercilessly against his.

"Mark   "

She saw his eyes for a moment before his mouth was pressed savagely against her own, dark eyes pitiless in their doubt and ruthlessly demanding in their desire. That one swift, bitter kiss seemed to last a lifetime. She felt it searing through her like a flame, burning and destroying, yet turning her heart to ice. There was nothing gentle or loverlike in Mark at that moment. He was all savage, the bitterness in him obliterating everything else.

She thrust her hands against him, pushing him from her·

"Let me go! I think   I think I must hate you!"

She knew that he could feel her trembling, and surely he must know that she still loved him? Was this, then, his way of revenge?

She heard him laugh.

"I might appreciate that better," he said, freeing her. "It would be a stronger passion than your lukewarm pity."

There was nothing she could say to him. The touch of his lips had awakened all her love, and although he had left it crushed and bruised, she could not deny it a second time. She could not tell him that her hatred would last.

He stood waiting, as if he half expected such an admission, and then he turned toward the door.

"If you let me know when you want the car on Thursday, I'll drive you down to York," he said.

"You don't need to do that, Mark." Her voice was unbelievably calm. "Heber can take me as far as the Fox and I can get the bus from there."

"I will be going to York in any case," he assured her "Thursday is their cattle market. I'm selling some of the Grange stock."

It was only a matter of convenience, after all. She tried

to laugh, but her voice sounded hollow and lost in her own ears. It was madness to imagine that Mark might have gone to York especially to see her safely onto the London train!

Martha Crosby came to "sleep in" the following day. She was a thin, sallow-skinned woman in her early fifties, with raven hair severely parted in the center and screwed up into two unbecoming plaits at the side of her head, and rather sad blue eyes. She had never been farther than the local market town for years, with the single exception of one never-to-be-forgotten day at Scarborough when she had spent all her time on the foreshore, bewildered by the gaudy array of cheap jewelry in the shops and the mounds of dressed crab and pink shrimps adorning the quayside stalls. She had stared fearfully into the glittering maw of an amusement arcade, fully convinced that she had stumbled, albeit unwittingly, upon the abode of the devil himself, and she had returned to Kirby Allerton with a description of her adventures that had amused the enlightened and deeply impressed her friends.

"Don't stay away too long," Harriet begged when Janet went to say goodbye. "I've got used to having you here, Janet."

"Don't worry," Janet said, stooping to kiss the wrinkled brow. "I'll get back just as quickly as I can, Mother Harriet."

Harriet's thin fingers clung a moment and the tired gray eyes lingered on Janet's face.

"It wouldn't be fair to keep you if you wanted to go," Harriet said as if in answer to some unspoken question of her own.

"I don't want to go," Janet assured her. "Not for always, Mother Harriet. It's just that I owe it to Charles Grantley to help him straighten out some of his aunt's affairs. You see," she added with the slow smile that many people found so attractive, "I was everything to Miss Pope   nurse, companion, secretary and confidante. The only thing I didn't know was that she had left me a little money in her will."

The letter from Miss Pope's lawyers had arrived the day before and the legacy was all quite official now.

"I'm sure it was because you deserved it," Harriet said. "But I'm selfish enough to hope it won't make you too independent so that you might not want to come back to Yorkshire."

"Whatever it does," Janet assured her, "it won't do that. If it's a fortune I'll bring you back a present!" she laughed.

When she turned, Mark was waiting at the door.

"Are you ready?" he asked.

"Yes." She drew on her gloves. "I don't think I've forgotten anything."

He crossed the room to take leave of his mother.

"I won't be long," he promised. "Martha will look after you till I get back."

He bent to kiss Harriet's cheek, and Janet felt an odd stirring at her heart. With his mother, at least, Mark was as gentle as he always had been. The love and respect that he had always shown toward her were mingled with pity now and a deep tenderness that might have seemed strange in him if Janet had not been able to remember the boy Mark who could never bear to see an animal hurt or a wild bird in distress.

The knowledge choked her throat with tears and she turned away to wait for him in the hall.

"I'm taking Jonathan," he announced. "He'll be safer under my eye."

"And less of an anxiety to your mother," Janet agreed.

"She does love him and worry about him, Mark."

"Yes," he said, but that was all.

Jonathan claimed the passenger seat in front of the car while Janet sat behind, trying to concentrate her attention on the familiar landscape as it slid by and not to think how wonderful it would be if this could be the way of the future for her and not just a day snatched from time to cling to passionately because it was not her own by right.

Mark and his child! They looked so alike sitting there that there could be no doubt about their close relationship. Jonathan had inherited all Mark's sturdy independence along with his unusual coloring, but the boy's soft lips were curved and parted innocently, while the man's mouth had hardened and become grimly bitter with the years.

Remembering its touch and the fiery intensity of Mark's kiss, she felt the hot color flooding into her cheeks, as it had done so many times in the past twenty-four hours, and when they reached York she was almost thankful that their journey had come to an end.

High up on the ridge of the moors, they had watched a gray pall of rain gathering over the city to wreathe the minster towers in a web of mist, and gradually it had spread over the wide vale, shutting out what little warmth remained in the October sun.

Mark seemed glad to get her to the station, although her train was not due for another half hour.

"Don't wait," she said awkwardly. "I know you must want to get away to the market so that you can get back to Wildfell as quickly as possible."

He hesitated.

"I thought we might have something to warm us up," he suggested. "A coffee, perhaps. Jonathan expects a lemonade at the end of a journey as a sort of right!"

Janet thanked him, almost absurdly grateful for his thoughtfulness, and he led the way to the Station Hotel.

Tall and broad-shouldered in his habitual garb of riding breeches and sports jacket, he commanded attention immediately. This, too, was a different Mark Langdon, assured and confident, profiting to a marked degree by the experience of the years he had spent away from the dale. There was nothing hesitant about him now, no youthful shyness in the presence of sophistication, no reticence as he mixed with the city crowd.

Janet found herself wondering about those years in London more than ever; wondering how Mark had lived his life there and how he could have absorbed the change so easily. It was obvious that it had been an entirely different life to have put such a polished seal on him. She tried not to think of it as a crust through which the old, spontaneous Mark would never break. Something seemed to have dried up inside him, leaving a bleakness that showed through in his eyes at times, although normally he kept it crushed down in case it might weaken his resolve to meet life with an indifference that would leave him invulnerable in future. He had told her that he would not let himself be hurt a second time, and she believed him determined to make absolutely sure.

Her heart aching at the thought, she found herself with little to say. It was absurd to feel that this parting was a shadow of things to come, absurd to be depressed by it, to let it make her feel nervous and confused when Mark spoke to her. She saw him looking at her once or twice, as if her restlessness irked him, and a good ten minutes before her train came in he called for his bill and rose to escort her on to the platform.

She had very little luggage, and he carried it himself, putting it down when they were through the barrier and

Jonathan was in proud possesion of the two platform tickets, which he fondly believed would take himself and Mark to London "another day."

"What name will your engine be?" he asked Janet excitedly, hopping from one foot to the other, his eyes never still as they darted among the groups of travelers on the platform. "All the big engines have names."

"Better wait and see," Mark advised. "There will be plenty of time when the train comes in."

"Where will it come from?"

"Edinburgh."

A pause.

"Where's that?"

"In Scotland."

"Oh?" Then, in a completely changed voice, "There's Mr. Ransome! He must be going to London, too."

Before either Mark or Janet could stop him he was speeding down the platform to greet his old friend. Janet felt the silence between herself and Mark growing until it stood between them like the gray pall of mist outside. She tried to say something, but what was there to say? Surely Mark could not expect her to apologize for Tom Ransome's presence in the station, although it was the kind of coincidence she would have liked to escape.

"Hello!" Tom greeted them rather sheepishly as Jonathan pulled him forward, clinging to his hand as if he half suspected a wish to escape. "It looks as if half the dale is on the way to London. I've just run into Bill Oxtoby and his wife, and Iris Middleton from the Bull."

"Janet is traveling alone," Mark said, "but no doubt you already know that." He turned to Janet, his eyes remote, his voice masked in ice as he concluded, "Now that you have company, Jonathan and I will push off. I want to get my buying done early."

The train was in sight, rounding the curve to come into the platform. He was cutting their farewell short by minutes, but he seemed determined to get away.

"Jonathan wanted to see the engine," Janet managed.

"Yes, please!" Jonathan begged, standing on tiptoe to kiss Janet with one eye on the advancing locomotive.

Mark held out his hand.

"I'll say goodbye, Janet." His formal handshake was shattering in its indifference to their parting. "You'll let me know, I suppose, if you decide to come back."

She had made him a promise, but he still thought her capable of changing her mind. His distrust of her was almost more than she could bear with protest. She watched him walk away along the platform, keeping pace with the engine for Jonathan's benefit, with the quick tears of disappointment gathering in her eyes.

Tom Ransome put a firm hand on her arm.

"Come on," he said, "I'll find you a corner seat."

When they were settled in their compartment the train was ready to move. Janet looked out at the deserted platform, and then, impulsively, she rose and hurried along the corridor to the first door. The signal lights were at green and the whistle blew. The train moved, gathering speed, and at the end of the platform a small boy stood looking after the engine, still awestruck by all he had seen.

Mark did not turn his head till Janet was almost level with them, and then, for an instant, she found herself looking straight into the depths of a man's troubled soul.

"Goodbye!" Jonathan shouted. "Goodbye! Come back soon."

Come back soon! Come back soon! The turning wheels seemed to grind the message out all the way to London, but it was not Mark's wish, but Jonathan's. What did Mark want of her? What did he really want?

In spite of her protest that she was far from hungry, Tom insisted that they should share a meal, but during the time they spent in the dining car, and even afterward he seemed to have curiously little to say. He seemed preoccupied with his own thoughts, and he did not tell her why he was going south or how long he expected to stay.

"What about the chickens while you're away?" she asked once when they were nearing the end of their journey. "Will Mrs. Bowes be able to cope?"

He seemed to bring his thought back from some considerable distance to answer her.

"Oh—yes, I hope so. I'm hoping that I won't have to sell up altogether, you see."

Janet looked surprised. It was little more than six weeks since Tom had set up at Kirby Allerton with such high hope for success in the future.

"But surely you won't make such a final decision so quickly?" she protested, knowing how proud he had been of his first small achievements.

Tom hesitated. His frank gaze suggested that he would have liked nothing better than to be able to confide in her, but the moment of indecision passed and a closed look clamped down on his suntanned face as he said, "Decisions are often made for us, Janet, whether we like them or not. I don't know what this decision will be, but it may rest with—my wife whether I come back to Kirby Allerton or not."

There was nothing more to be said, Janet realized, but she shook Tom's hand on parting a little more warmly than she would have done in ordinary circumstances and was glad when he said that he hoped they would meet again.

Charles Grantley was at the ticket barrier.

"I've got my car," he said, taking Janet's arm and glancing at Tom. "Can we give your friend a lift?"

Tom thanked him and shook his head.

"I may have to catch a plane direct to Zürich," he explained.

Janet remembered that he had told her his wife was in Switzerland, and the thought of Tom making what was obviously an unhappy and decisive journey worried her even after Charles began to discuss her own affairs.

"I think you have better be prepared for it, Janet," he said, looking down at her with a teasing smile that was so essentially Charles. "You're going to be a comparatively wealthy woman when we reach the final settlement of my aunt's estate. Aunt Emily, apparently, never did things in a small way. She bought in bulk, and that applied to bonds and shares as simply as it did to sugar and tea. Aunt Emily liked plenty of everything."

"But, Charles," Janet protested, "none of all this can really apply to me. We were not even related."

"She was very fond of you," Charles assured her, guiding his expensive car through the heavy traffic of the Euston Road. "And that is much the same thing. Besides, she was not related to anyone except me. Aunt Emily was my mother's only sister, and she never married. I think she secretly longed for a daughter, though, or even a niece. She had her unpredictable side, like a good many other people. She never discussed her great wealth with anyone but her lawyer. Even I didn't know what the old lady was worth till she died."

Janet listened abstractedly. Her mind would not quite take in the fact that she had been left a considerable amount of money by an old lady who had engaged her six years ago for her companionship and the care she could give her in the last years of her life. It seemed unlikely when she had always considered Charles as Miss Pope's sole heir and beneficiary under her will.

It seemed now that Charles was offering her a new life.

"You needn't feel that you are marrying me for my money now, Janet!" he grinned. "You can do anything you like with your life, but I still want you to share it with me. Of course, this makes you entirely independent. You can go where you like, do what you like. You can even keep on the villa at St. Jean."

Janet thought of the lovely little villa on the shores of the smiling Mediterranean, and then the thought of lonely Wildfell, standing squarely on the fells, facing the onslaught of every wind that blew, crashed in on her mind. She had the choice of two homes, and there was no doubt in her heart which she would chose.

"I wouldn't have any use for the villa, Charles," she said. "It would only be eating its head off down there while we were here in England."

"Which means that you still refuse to marry me?"

"It means that I don't think we should keep the villa. It has outlived its usefulness. Your aunt liked to be there because of the climate and her rheumatism, but I have no duties in France."

"But plenty in Yorkshire?"

She looked at him squarely.

"Yes, Charles."

"Is it—the hill farmer?"

She felt her cheeks burn.

"No."

"What then?"

"I have promised to look after his mother and—there's my quite genuine love of the dale."

He made a small impatient sound in his throat.

"Marriageable women have been known to fritter

away their lives looking after a succession of old ladies, Janet," he warned. "I shall break down the barrier of that absurd dale of yours in time. Surely someone else can be found to look after Langdon's mother?"

"Not at the moment." Her voice was firm. "It is my job, and the only person who could take it from me is Ruth."

"Mrs. Langdon's own daughter? What took her to Canada?"

"I don't know. Young people emigrate for a score of reasons. I don't know why Ruth went away," Janet confessed.

"You could write to her and ask her to come back," he suggested.

"Yes, I suppose I could." The idea had been lying dormant in Janet's mind for a long time, but when she had mentioned Ruth to Mark she had always come more directly up against the barrier of reserve that she had never been able to scale. "I'm sure she must want to come," she mused.

"Daughters are strange creatures sometimes," Charles observed. "Perhaps Mrs. Langdon has found a great deal of recompense in you."

"I don't think you would feel that if you had known Ruth," Janet told him quietly. "And I don't think she could have changed."

Always, when she thought of change, she remembered Mark, but Ruth and Mark were different. Ruth had been gentle and pliable, and it had always been a surprising thing to Janet that she had finally left the dale to seek a life of her own away from her father's domination.

As if Charles was determined to bring about the change in her own heart that he had so cheerfully predicted in the shortest space of time, he rushed her around London in a hectic round of amusement calculated to sweep any girl off her feet. In his heart of hearts he knew that Janet would not be easily swayed, but he was also banking on her own changed financial circumstances to help him to his heart's desire. He considered that no girl, however conscientious she might be, would deliberately bury herself in a remote hill farm where the living was as primitive as a sadistic man could make it. He had not liked Mark Langdon at their meeting and nothing had happened to make him change his mind. Mark's scowling disregard of him had not been the only cause. Charles had been far more disturbed by the look in Janet's eyes when Mark's name was mentioned, although he wondered hopefully if Mark might not have hurt her now to the point of disillusionment.

When he took her to his aunt's lawyers, he arranged, as unobtrusively as possible, for an advance sum of money to be paid over to her, and Janet accepted the check without the slightest idea what she was going to do with it. This was all new and rather painful to her. She had not quite accepted Miss Pope's death yet, and to spend the old lady's money as liberally as Charles suggested seemed all wrong to her.

"There *are* a few things I would like to buy," she agreed when she began to think about her return to Yorkshire. "Things we'll need for the winter at Windfell, and something for Jonathan."

She had not mentioned Mark, and she supposed that he would not accept a present from her.

She did not allow the thought to damp her enthusiasm for her other purchase, however, and spent a whole afternoon around Regent Street shopping for essentials for herself and little luxuries for Harriet, which gave her far more pleasure. If the rather elaborate bed jacket she bought with its narrow rows of soft white fur was more

suited to a Mayfair boudoir than Harriet's modest room
at the farm, she did not give the fact a second thought. It
was something she wanted to do for the woman who had
done so much for her and whom she had repaid with
thoughtlessness for six long years.

Never quite able to get the sense of her own ingratitude
out of her mind, she would not delay her journey back to
Yorkshire for a moment longer than was absolutely necessary. Charles reasoned and even pleaded with her, but
after the last document was signed and Miss Pope's lawyer had shaken her by the hand and wished her happiness
in the future with the detached air of all the legal profes-
sion once a client has been passed successfully out of the
inner sanctum, she said that she must go.

"You're not going to pass up our celebration dinner?"
Charles asked, astounded. "I've got everything arranged."

"If it's arranged for this evening I won't desert you,"
she told him, "but I must get the first train home
tomorrow."

It was that one word "home" that dismayed Charles
more than anything else. He made the evening perfect for
her, and Janet, in the new silk dress she had bought that
afternoon after a good deal of hesitation and doubt about
its suitability for the future, thoroughly enjoyed herself.

It might have been the effect of the wine Charles
ordered that flushed her cheeks and left her eyes like stars
in a dark firmament, or it might just have been the
thought of her return to Wildfell, but Charles Grantley
acknowledged that he had never seen her looking lovelier,
nor so desirable.

He saw her onto the York train next morning with the
utmost reluctance, but he never doubted for one moment
that she would come back.

Janet had written to Wildfell, but she did not expect to

be met till she reached the Fox and Hare. Mark would probably send Heber over with the car because there was no other means of transportation to the farm.

When the train drew alongside the platform at York she was standing at the carriage window. Her numerous parcels and packages demanded the services of a porter, and she smiled as she remembered Charles's parting sally.

"You look completely 'up from the country,' Janet! I've never seen so many parcels and odd bits and pieces since Aunt Emily got loose in Venice that afternoon and decided to buy glass!"

It was amazing how elusive English porters could be when one considered their counterparts on the Continent, she mused, looking down the platform, and then her heart almost stopped beating as she saw Mark.

He came striding toward her, head and shoulders above the passengers already spilling from the train, and her heart bounded once again, fast and excited in the knowledge that he had come to meet her.

"I had to come to York," he explained, signaling for a porter to collect her luggage. "I had some business to attend to, and my mother got your letter just before I left."

Janet tried not to feel damped by his reason for coming.

"How is she?" she asked. "I hope she's been all right while I've been away."

"I think she missed you," he acknowledged briefly, "but she's been much the same as usual."

"I'm sorry about all the parcels," she apologized as he began to pick them up. "I seem to have bought rather a lot."

"I think we should be able to cope," he said, leading the way through the ticket barrier. "Have you had anything to eat?"

"I had lunch on the train. I knew I wouldn't get anything in the local train between York and Pickering, so I had it early."

"If this train had been late you would have missed your connection and had two hours to wait."

He had not asked if she had enjoyed her visit to London or what had brought her back to Yorkshire so soon, but his habitual cynicism had deserted him for the moment and he seemed almost companionable.

"Is Jonathan with you?" she asked eagerly.

"No. I thought it advisable to leave him at home on this occasion."

They had arrived at the parking lot and Janet looked around her for the familiar old Morris. It was nowhere to be seen, and Mark was striding toward a shining new limousine drawn up in a corner.

"Mark!" she exclaimed. "You've got a new car?"

He smiled one-sidedly.

"Don't you think it was about time?" he observed dryly.

"But it—it's magnificent!"

"We'll have to keep it at the Grange," he said. "It would only make Wildfell appear more derelict than ever."

"It needn't be derelict, Mark," she said gently. "It's only grown that way because—because you didn't care. It used to be a comfortable enough home. It was only the conditions that were hard."

"They still are," he pointed out grimly. "I wonder you came back to them."

"I wanted to come." She settled herself in the passenger seat of the roomy new car, feeling suddenly that Mark had taken a first step along the return road to his old self. "London's too big and too busy for me."

"You may change your mind," he suggested, stacking

parcels on the back seat. "You seem to have bought half of Oxford Street!"

"Well, at least a quarter of Regent Street!" she laughed, feeling like a prisoner who has suddenly and inexplicably been set free. "There were so many things I wanted to bring back!"

The car slid away and she sank luxuriously into the comfortable leather upholstery. It was a golden journey, driving out along the moorland roads on a day like this when the wind blew freshly and there was not a cloud in sight. Vast tracks of azure sky stretched to infinity, and the rolling landscape beneath it seemed part of another world. All the bright glory of autumn still lingered in the hedgerows and the woods, russet and saffron and gold, like the rich colors in an artist's palette after he had painted his masterpiece.

Mark seemed in a mood to match the day, mellowed and content to drive at the restricted speed a new engine demanded, in no great hurry to be home.

"We'll go around by the Grange," he suggested. "I've something to see down there."

Janet felt her heart beating close against her throat. Mark had never suggested that she might go to the Grange before. She had supposed it to be closed territory as far as she was concerned, and now he was offering to take her there.

"There's been trouble with the roof," he explained as he steered the car between the massive stone gateposts, "and I want it seen to before the winter comes in earnest."

He unlocked the main door and they went into the deserted hall. It was still lovely, Janet thought, and as they walked through the rooms she could imagine the beautiful home it must have been and felt doubly sorry for Tom Ransome in consequence. She could not mention Tom however.

"I've thought of bringing my mother down here," Mark explained their visit. "It's warmer than our higher reaches of the moor and—more comfortable."

It was the first time he had ever made any concession to material comfort, Janet realized, or conceded the fact that Wildfell was not all it should be.

"It would be wonderful for her," she agreed enthusiastically.

"And for you?"

She flushed scarlet.

"Do I come into it? I am only here to look after your mother and Jonathan," she said.

Mark did not argue the point, closing the door of what had been the Ransomes' very handsome drawing room with an abrupt movement that indicated that the discussion was at an end.

"I thought it might obviate the need for worry if she came down here," he said. "If we are cut off by snow during the winter, the dale road is always opened first."

"Would you stay at Wildfell if your mother came here?" she asked, her heart thumping fast as he turned to lock the main door.

"I think so," he said. "It has always been my home."

She had always known Mark felt that way about Wildfell, but perhaps he was also glad to put the length of the dale between them. The step back to the past must have been a vain hope of her own imagining.

Depressed by the conviction, she climbed back into the car and they drove in silence to the farm on the ridge of the moor.

As if in deliberate contrast to the Grange, Wildfell presented a sullen face. The weathered stone itself was beautiful, but the woodwork and outbuildings needed a fresh coat of paint and the scene in the yard was chaotic.

It had rained heavily the day before and there was a great deal of mud around, which had been carried into the house by a steady procession of feet. Janet drew in a resigned breath at the thought of the work involved in cleaning it all up. It occurred to her that there were a great many odds and ends lying around, together with a general warmth that had never been connected with Wildfell before.

Mark crossed to the kitchen door. He opened it, but he did not go in, and Janet noticed a lightness about the dungeonlike room that completely transformed it. The old black range had gone.

"Mark!" she cried, crossing to the gleaming cream-and-chromium coal-burning stove. "However did you do it—in three days?"

"People have been obliging," he said almost gruffly. "I saw it in Pickering when I was down there last week. We need hot water around the place and a more efficient way of cooking."

A stove and a bathroom! They were the necessities of life, Janet supposed, and although there could be nothing personal in the fact that Mark has seen fit to install them at Wildfell at last, she hugged the fact to her as a sign of change.

CHAPTER SIX

IN SPITE OF MARK'S offer of a more comfortable way of living, Harriet Langdon refused to be transferred to the Grange.

"I'm well enough here, where I belong, Mark," she said. "Wildfell has been my home for over thirty years and it would be a foolish uprooting to change it now. I've weathered plenty of winters up here on the moor; this one will be no different from the rest, if I'm called to weather it, too."

Janet tried not to think that there had been doubt in Harriet's voice. Looking at her, she could not see any outward sign of change. It was only that there did not appear to be any obvious progress, either. Harriet seemed to be marking time, waiting for something, perhaps.

The thought of Ruth was never far from Janet's mind, but she hesitated to ask Mark to write to his sister. It was the sort of thing he would decide for himself.

When she had returned from London she had distributed her gifts, and Harriet wore her new bed jacket on Sunday mornings and when the doctor was expected, folding it away carefully between times in case it should not last. She had never been the possessor of such a delicately lovely thing in all her life before, and she handled it with awe.

Janet made new curtains for her window and extra cushions for her chair, sewing them lovingly by hand in the long evenings after the lamps were lighted but she dared not suggest similar improvements in any of the other rooms, even with Mark in this more amenable mood. These new luxuries were permitted for his mother, but not for him. He spent the hours of darkness mainly in the cheerless houseplace or at work on the endless forms and accounts that had to be kept, and during the day he was always on the moor.

Martha Crosby had departed for Kirby Allerton, promising to come again if she was needed.

"With all that fine hot water and little enough to do about the house," she remarked as she took her leave, "you'll not be needin' help. Unless it was an emergency," she had added to Janet on their way to the door with a look in the direction of Harriet's room.

Janet did not want to think about emergencies. She was happier than she had ever been, and the days passed in a blessed eventlessness that added to their peace.

More than once she climbed with Jonathan onto the moor where Mark and Heber were dressing the ewes' feet or seeing to the long, dry stone dikes before the winter set in, and on these occasions she was quite content to live the hours individually, without thought of the future.

It was five weeks before she saw Tom Ransome again, and then only because she went to Kirby Allerton for some thread to complete her sewing.

Tom strode down the main street toward her, something in the buoyancy of his step and the expression of his brown eyes making him look years younger and more like the Tom she had first known.

"I've been wondering when I was going to meet you," he said by way of greeting. "If I hadn't met Martha Crosby and heard you were back at Wildfell I would have sworn you had deserted us to remain in London!"

"I've been back for weeks," Janet told him. "London didn't hold me as long as it did you, apparently!"

A shadow crossed his face and the smile faded from his eyes.

"It wasn't London," he said. "I've been abroad all this time."

She looked up at him, seeing the obvious signs of strain in his face now that they were nearer.

"I'm sorry, Tom," she said. "The situation hasn't changed, I gather?"

He drew in a deep breath.

"It has changed so drastically," he said, "that's it difficult to believe. Poor Lucia! She was so utterly pathetic at the last. She had no idea what her illness was until a few weeks ago, and even then she was convinced that she would recover. She had never had any trouble with her lungs before, but she had lived hard. How hard I don't think anyone will ever know. She burned herself up trying to succeed, and she loved a gay life."

"When did she die?" Stunned by the news, Janet was aware that Tom was genuinely sorry about his wife's death, even though she had made living difficult for him for six years.

"A week ago. It happened suddenly at the end. I had been with her the day before, and she had seemed brighter and most eager to be up and around. It was against doctor's orders, of course, but after I left she had taken the law into her own hands and gone out onto the balcony on her own. It was a glorious evening, with the snow already fallen on the highest peaks of the Alps, but the air was treacherous. A fit of coughing ended it all. She was dead when they found her an hour later."

She knew that Tom would never think of his wife's death as a happy release for himself, even though his impulsive marriage had gone wrong from the beginning. He was much more likely to blame himself for its dismal failure, wondering unhappily where he had taken the first false step. In his heart of hearts he might acknowledge his wife's frailness of character, but he had too much compassion and kindliness in his makeup to speak of it now.

They walked a little way along the road in silence.

"Will you stay in Allerton now, Tom?" Janet asked at last.

He seemed to hesitate.

"I want to stay," he said. "It has always been my home. When I was younger I never thought of anything but settling down in the dale. It's strange," he mused after a pause, "how things turn out. You plan your life, seeing it all set out before you with never a cloud in the sky, and then, out of nowhere, comes change. You're restless or something goes wrong—some trivial thing—and you make a snap decision that turns the future upside down. I wonder how many people have their own impulsive waywardness to thank for the mess they make of their lives?"

Was he thinking about Ruth, regretting that he had not married his childhood sweetheart?

"Sometimes we get a second chance, Tom."

Janet had spoken impulsively and he turned sharply to look at her.

"Do you believe that?" he demanded.

"I've seen it happen."

"And it always works out   happily?"

"Not always." Mark's name flashed across her mind and her lips quivered. "It depends on the two people involved. Whether they are able to forgive or not."

He looked beyond her, his gaze resting on the gray bulk of Parson's Crag which looked across the ridge to Wildfell.

"There are some unforgivable things in life, Janet," he said. "Deep hurts that youth inflicts and learns about afterward in an agony of regret."

She felt that he wanted to speak about the past but could not bring himself to discuss it so soon after his wife's death.

"I think you should stay in the dale," she said. "You've started again, Tom, and this is where you wanted to be."

"Yes," he agreed, drawing in a long breath. "I've thought about it for years. I didn't make my decision hastily."

He walked with her to the beginning of the dale road, and when she had mounted her bicycle she imagined that he had let her go reluctantly.

Thinking about Tom and the past, she was soon at Wildfell, with Jonathan rushing out to greet her and the sheep dogs barking their noisy welcome at the gate. This was the sort of background Tom wanted, she thought. The gentle peace of the hills, a child's laughter, the time-lessness of quiet days. It was the life he had always known and the life he had returned to find, but, like herself, he would not feel it complete without love.

Once again she felt herself drawn in deepest sympathy and understanding to this man who had come back, as she had done, to make a fresh start, to wipe out the years between, if that was possible.

"We're going to have our tea early!" Jonathan cried excitely. "An' then there's a s'prise!"

"For you?" Janet asked

He shook his head.

"It's a family s'prise."

Mark came around the end of the stable buildings at that moment. He appeared to have been working there all afternoon.

"I'll hurry tea," Janet said. "Will you come in for it, Mark?"

He so rarely did that she expected him to refuse.

"Please!" Jonathan begged. "Then we can all see the s'prise. It came in a big truck," he added excitedly for Janet's benefit, "an' it has lots an' lots of wire!"

Mark laughed.

"You're not going to impress Janet with a gasoline engine for making electric light," he said. "It's your grandmother who is going to be excited."

"Oh, Mark, that's wonderful!" Janet exclaimed. "Your mother could even have a television set. It would pass so very many happy hours for her."

"I'd thought of that," he said. When he spoke of his mother or produced anything to ease the burden of her long confinement to her room, all the bitterness and harshness went out of his face. "We'll have to get the lighting fixed up first, though. I've run a temporary circuit into the house to please Jonathan, and we'll have an official switch-on after tea. One table lamp will be quite as effective as a row of illuminations, I expect. He's been watching the progress of the work all afternoon."

The family atmosphere had suddenly deepened and Janet held the knowledge close against her heart as she busied herself with the simple meal. Jonathan fetched and carried for her, dropping a plate of buttered scones on the stone flags of the house place. The collies eyed them hopefully.

"All right!" Janet laughed. "You can have them! They're not going to look exactly decorative on the table with half the butter stuck on the houseplace floor!"

Her laughter was full and eager, with all the sudden joy in her heart bubbling to the surface because for the first time the mask of indifference that shrouded Mark's eyes had been lifted and he seemed to have admitted her to his comradeship.

It was a happy meal, rounded off by the dramatic moment when the electric table lamp was switched on. The little pool of yellow light drew them closely together, and they sat around it in a compact group: the old lady with silvering hair, her thin hands folded idly on the plaid rug covering her knees; the tall, darkly tanned man with the look of the open air about him; the girl beside him, lovely and tender in her young womanhood with only a hint of wistfulness in her blue eyes, and the eagerly excited child plying them with questions about the new light.

Janet did not want to break up that happy scene, but soon it was Jonathan's bedtime and Mark had tacitly agreed that a regular time should be adhered to even on special occasions such as this.

"Will I have a light soon?" Jonathan asked on his way upstairs. "Is it going to be in all the house?"

"As soon as I have time to see to it," Mark promised.

When Janet had settled Harriet for the night, with the new lamp to read by for half an hour until she fell asleep, she went into the kitchen to wash the dishes and prepare Mark's supper. The new stove had halved her former work, but she was still shy about expressing her gratitude. Mark had almost gone out of his way to prove that there was nothing personal about these innovations, and even with them the work at Wildfell was still hard and exacting. It was easier, however, to keep a meal hot when there was some distant job on hand and she had no idea when the men would return, and the kitchen was always warm nowadays. Clothes that had been soaked through on the open moor were dried more quickly, and muddy boots were more easily cleaned.

She took up a pair of Jonathan's boots, scraping the dried earth from them into the sink. It was still the huge, shallow stone affair she remembered as a child where Ruth and she had sat to wash their feet before they raced each other up to bed. She wondered about Ruth so often these days, and always behind these thoughts was the thought of Harriet.

Before Mark came in she tiptoed to his mother's door. The new light was still burning, but Harriet Langdon had fallen asleep.

Janet crossed quietly to the bedside, looking down on the still face for a moment before she turned away. Then, in a second of strange panic, she lifted the lamp and held it close to the bed. Her heart thumped loudly and her breath was caught in her throat, but presently Harriet moved and sighed.

With trembling fingers Janet switched off the light. The little incident had unnerved her out of all proportion, and she could not thrust the memory of her fear aside even when Mark came in.

"I'll get your supper," she said. "It's ready."

He looked around at her, sensing her uneasiness.

"What's worrying you, Janet?" he asked abruptly.

"I was thinking about Ruth," she said. "Is there no way of getting her to come home, Mark?"

His face darkened, the mouth firming into the old, hard lines that made him look years older than he really was.

"Ruth is trying to make a new life for herself in Canada," he said. "We have no right to ask her to come back."

"It was because of your mother," she explained. "I thought if I had Ruth's address I might write to her."

She knew that Ruth had written to him quite recently, a lively, cheerful letter that Harriet had folded away beneath her pillow but which Mark had read in silence.

"I can do that," he said almost curtly. "Ruth is kept in touch with most of the family news."

After a small, awkward silence she said, without quite knowing why, "I met Tom Ransome this afternoon in Allerton. He has been abroad for the past five weeks."

Instantly Mark stiffened, his whole body drawn up as if to combat an enemy.

"I wonder if it will surprise you to know that I am not interested in Tom Ransome's travels around the world?" he said icily.

"You used to be friends, Mark." Janet's heart was beating swiftly, so swiftly that it seemed to drive the words between her parted lips in a tumult of appeal. "You were the closest of friends at one time. I can't see that Tom has done anything to injure you. He has had his own share of unhappiness. I'm not sure whether you know about it or not, but now that his wife is dead and he has come back to Allerton, I think he should be allowed to settle in peace."

He swung around to confront her, his eyes blazing, his mouth cruelly compressed. For a moment he looked as if he might strike her, and then the mask that he had worn for so long was down again and he gazed beyond her to the table she had set so happily a few minutes before.

"Treachery is a thing I could never understand," he said coldly. "I've told you what I feel about Ransome, and I repeat now that I will not have any friendship between him and anyone living under my roof. If he wants Ruth's address," he added cuttingly, "let him ask for it from me."

Aghast, Janet remembered her own questions about Ruth, and now it seemed that Mark believed she had been asking on Tom's behalf. Well, what if she had? Tom was free now. He had every right to ask for Ruth's address if he wanted it.

Even as she took up the challenge she knew that the issue went deeper than that, deeper even than her own integrity where Mark's wishes were concerned.

"Mark," she begged, making a desperate sort of effort to reach him even through the concealing mask, "what is it? What has made you like this?"

His closed, tensed face gave her no answer.

"I couldn't expect you to understand," he told her. "But I want you to realize, Janet, that you will have to leave Comerdale if your friendship with Ransome continues."

She wanted to point out how unjust such a decision was, that it was unfair to both of them when he would not offer her a fuller explanation, but something about him, something in the still, cold fury of his face held her back, silencing her even as he left her standing there in the warmth of what she had so fondly believed might one day be a friendly room.

When midnight had struck and he had not returned she went heavily toward the stairs. There was no need to wait any longer. His meal remained untouched and the house seemed empty. Heber and the cowman had gone to their own quarters long ago.

She lay awake, listening in the stillness, and then it seemed that there was a movement on the stairs. Stretched taut on her bed, she waited for Mark's footsteps to pass her door, and then she heard his voice, quiet and saddened.

"Janet, can you come? My mother is asking for you."

He had been with Harriet. Trembling, Janet felt for her dressing gown, thrusting her feet into the warm slippers she had bought in London, and turned to the door. When she opened it Mark came in. He seemed to look about the room dazedly at first, taking in its bareness.

"I've sent Heber for the doctor," he said, "but I doubt if he will get here in time."

She put her hand over his.

"Mark—don't worry," she said in a strangled whisper.

He followed her down the stairs in silence, his face haggard, his mouth twisted in a grim line. The new lamp at his mother's bedside threw it up into sharp relief. It was still a hard face, but the bitterness had gone.

Harriet lay with her head back on her pillows. She looked very small and frail in the yellow glow from the lamp and her eyes seemed to be fixed on something beyond them.

"Ah, Janet!" she said when Janet came forward into the light. "You've come back?"

"Yes, Mother Harriet, I've come back to stay."

Her fingers fastened over the thin, listless hand on the pink coverlet and she was glad when she saw the relief that flooded into Harriet's eyes. It did not matter what Mark thought now.

"It isn't an easy place, isn't Wildfell." Harriet had lapsed into the warm idiom of her youth. "But Mark will do his best. Be patient with him, Janet."

Mark turned abruptly to the fire, standing leaning on the high mantelpiece with his head down against it and his hand shielding his eyes.

His mother's eyes were closed. She lay with Janet's fingers clasped in hers for a long time, breathing shallowly.

"Ruth?" The fingers in Janet's tightened. "You'll stay, Ruth, now that you've come home?"

"Yes, mother...."

Janet's voice choked on the word and she could not utter the last part of the familiar name. She sat quite still as Mark moved back to the bed, and then she felt the pressure on her hand relax and Harriet Langdon was dead.

It was so gentle a passing, so quiet that she could hardly regret it. Harriet, whose life had not been easy, had been allowed to end it in peace.

Mark stood for a long time by the bed, and Janet left him there. He did not seem to need her now. He did not seem to need anyone.

"If only Ruth had been here," she said when they met the following morning.

He looked at her steadily.

"Ruth must come back to Wildfell of her own accord," he said. "Not by any urging of yours or mine."

Even at this stage she was prompted to dig beneath the hard crust of his reserve in search of the man she had once known.

"Is that because of your pride, Mark? Is it because you think that Ruth should never have gone away?" she asked. "I know you were bitter about me, but surely Ruth was different."

He stood looking at her in the gray light of early morning, and for a moment she thought that the wall he had erected about his heart would crumble. Then he spoke deliberately and remotely about their former love.

"I followed you to London six years ago, Janet, but I never contacted you. I called myself a fool for going, and I vowed never to see you again. Then something happened that changed my life completely, and I came back to Comerdale determined to live it as remotely as possible, in my own way. I have been trying to do that now for over three years, with what measure of success or failure I leave you to guess."

It was a bitter speech, and she could not answer it.

IN THE DAYS THAT FOLLOWED she felt that the past was dead. Mark had loved someone else and what had been between herself and him was forgotten. He had said as much, and his every action since she had come back to the dale seemed to prove it. He had no interest in her apart from the fact that she had cared for his mother and Jonathan.

Now that Harriet Langdon was dead she was faced with the fact that she was alone at Wildfell with Mark, virtually his housekeeper and still in love with him.

Martha Crosby had come to clear up after the funeral, but she could not stay. She was likely to be married, she announced with a queer mixture of embarrassment and pride, and she had to get her own house in order. Folks would talk, she supposed, but she had known Herbert Smiles for over forty years and he was a respectable widower.

Janet clung to Martha as long as she could. It was almost as if the older woman stood as a buffer between herself and Mark, fending off the issue of the future.

"I'll have to go before Christmas," Martha informed her one day, and the next, when Janet returned from Kirby Allerton, she had gone.

"But why?" Janet asked, bewildered, when Mark broke the news to her. "She had plenty of time, even if she had wanted to get home before Christmas."

Mark did not reply. He stood looking at her for several minutes, as if he was weighing up a situation that had become intolerable to them both.

"You've been holding on to Martha Crosby for three weeks now, Janet," he observed at last. "She was bound to go one day."

"Yes," she agreed flatly, "I suppose so."

Mark seemed to sense her thoughts, and for a moment

she imagined that he was going to laugh. She could not
have stood his derision, but she was wholly unprepared
for his savagery.

"The situation needn't alarm you," he said harshly.
"You are quite safe where I am concerned. I brought you
here to look after my mother and to care for Jonathan,
and I don't intend you to leave until I have made other
arrangements for the child. When he is old enough to go
to school, that will be arranged, too."

Pale and shaken, Janet turned away, unable to argue
any more because her heart felt dead.

The following morning Mark removed himself to the
Grange, lock, stock and barrel.

It was a temporary measure, she supposed, until he
could find someone to act as her successor. Her usefulness to Mark was almost at an end.

Stunned and unhappy, she tried to make the new situation seem as natural as possible to Jonathan, but his
questions caught her unaware so often that she thought
even the child must guess her secret love.

It was a mild December, and Jonathan was still riding
his pony along the beck and sometimes up onto the wilder
side of the fell. On these excursions Janet usually accom-
panied him on foot, but sometimes she took her bicycle
and Jonathan would gallop down over the dead heather
while she cycled swiftly along the winding road to catch
up with him. If Mark saw them on any of these excursions
he generally managed to keep out of their way. He saw
Jonathan at Wildfell at the end of each day, but he would
not wait after the child had been put to bed.

Jonathan missed him and was more difficult to handle
in consequence. He wanted to know why they had not all
been removed to the Grange so that they could be
together.

By the second week in December it became too cold for the high reaches of the moor and they rode toward Kirby Allerton. Here, one morning, they met Tom again. He had bought himself a horse, a lovely dappled gray with nice manners and a gentle way with children, and Jonathan immediately attached himself to the newcomer. He longed to get up on that sleek silver back, and his joy was complete when Tom let him ride to the top of the dale, leading the pony by his side.

It was the first of several meetings. Tom, somehow, was always there on the ridge when they rode toward Allerton, and the friendship was so easy and so happy that Janet could not snub him or refuse Jonathan the joy of going that way again in the hope that they would meet. A strong attachment had developed between the boy and the man, and quite often Janet surprised Tom looking at the child with a world of longing in his eyes.

It was nearing Christmas, and Janet, faced with the prospect of the festivities generally associated with that happy season, wondered what would happen at Wildfell.

It was Tom who first mentioned a Christmas tree.

"Let me bring you one up from my property," he offered, but Janet, thinking of all the firs at the Grange that Jonathan declared were "just the right height for a Christmas tree," hesitated to accept the offer.

"I'm hoping Mark will bring one," she said. "Surely he can't be so busy that he'll forget it's Christmas."

Tom frowned.

"No," he said vaguely. "Most things are forgiven and forgotten at Christmas. I always thought it was the nicest idea in the world."

They were riding toward the dale, over the ridge, and when Wildfell came in sight he looked up and reined in his horse.

"I wish it were possible for us to spend Christmas together, Janet," he said. "We're like the proverbial happy family—you and me and Jonathan! A child makes Christmas." He drew a deep breath. "There's—something I've been going to ask you for days," he added. "You can say no if you don't want to do it and I'll understand. Will you give me Ruth's address?"

The hot color ran up into Janet's cheeks in an embarrassed flood.

"All right," he said before she could answer him. "I see that you can't. Don't worry about it, Janet. The decision wasn't yours."

He turned his horse's head and left them rather abruptly, but she knew that he understood.

They reached the farm, and Heber came grumbling to open the paddock gate.

"Pity ye haven't more to do than ride t'moors on a day like this," he observed ungraciously. "T'maister be fair flayed wi' anger when he seed ye up there wi' young Ransome. He'd come wi' tree for lad, an' there ye were, away gallivantin' wi't'other one!"

"Be quiet, Heber!" Janet said sharply, dismayed at having missed Mark. "What have you done with the tree?"

"It be flung doon i' the house place where it were left," Heber informed her in a huff. "Ah took nae dealin' wi' it whatever. Like as not t'maister hae flayed me if Ah'd opened my mouth."

Disappointment flowed over Janet like an engulfing tide. Mark had made this gesture and she had not been there to receive it. She wondered if she should go to the Grange and tell him how sorry she was, and then she asked herself if it would really matter to him. Heber exaggerated these little domestic incidents to such an extent that it was difficult to decide where the truth ended and imagination began. Mark had brought the tree and left it in the house place. When he came later in the evening to see Jonathan she would thank him for it on Jonathan's behalf.

But Mark did not come. The light faded and a harsh northerly wind began to blow. It held the first bite of winter in its teeth, and when she went to the door of the house place to look out the sky was gray with sullen cloud.

Heber, too, had disappeared, and when she spoke to the cowman he said that "like as not t'other two would be out on t'hill gathering down t'sheep."

Janet went to bed with an uneasy feeling that night. It was not because she was in the house alone, with only a child for company. She was too much of a countrywoman to be frightened on that account, nor did the banshee wailing of a northeast wind driving sleet before it from the sea unduly alarm her. A strange premonition of events marching inexorably beyond her control had taken possession of her, chilling her heart and making sleep impossible.

She lay awake listening to the wind, and when Heber came home with the first light she leaned from her bedroom window and peered down into the yard, expecting Mark to be with him.

"Heber," she called, "go into the house place and I'll get you something warm to drink."

The old man looked up at her, grunted and nodded. In spite of his complaining ways he was faithful and a hard worker when occasion demanded, and Mark had said that he could not be done without.

"Is—the master coming?" she asked, using the term the men always applied to Mark. "He must be soaked through."

"Ay, he be that an' no mistak'," Heber agreed, settling himself in front of the stove. "But he b'aint comin'. 'No,' he said, 'off ye gan, Heber, an'warm thissen at t'stove. Ah be well enough at Grange.' An' off he went, soaked an' fair flayed wi' weariness, to walk four miles t'Grange. Maybe if there warn't a woman about t'place," he added, looking across the hearth accusingly, "he'd 'ave cum. He wants nae truck wi' women, disn't t'maister."

"All right, Heber," Janet said. "Drink your coffee. Do you want anything to eat? There is a bit of pie in the oven and some potatoes."

The old shepherd didn't need a second bidding. She left him eating heartily while she went back to bed and lay thinking about Mark walking those four extra miles to the Grange because she was here at Wildfell.

I've got to go, she thought. *The Grange is comfortable enought, but this is nearer to Mark's work and it is his home.*

Once the decision was made she accepted it. The heaviness in her heart was like lead, but it was no new thing. It had been there for weeks, the inevitable ending of her love.

When she rose at last, it was full daylight, a gray day with a cutting wind whipping over the fells and rising to fury on the open moor.

Mark and Heber had brought most of the sheep down onto the more sheltered reaches of the dale, and the stragglers would be gathered during the day. The heavy sky foretold snow, and by eleven o'clock, when the mail came, it was bitterly cold. Janet put a coat on to go to the gate for the letters.

To her surprise the mailman was coming toward her up the path.

"What's happened to the mailbox?" she asked, smiling. "Has it blown away in last night's gale?"

"Box be all right," the mailman assured her. "It be this 'ere cable. They've to be delivered in person." He turned the small envelope over in his gloved hand, examining it with unabashed curiosity. "I understand as how it's from Canada," he announced. "It's for Mr. Langdon."

Janet's heart was beating swiftly as she took the envelope.

"I'll see that he gets it," she said.

She supposed that she could have asked the mailman to redeliver Mark's mail to the Grange, but he was an old man and he had just come up the dale. It was not yet common knowledge that Mark had removed himself to the Grange and she was not going to be the means of giving the gossip to the entire countryside.

With Jonathan in tow, she made the journey to Scarton in the teeth of one of the fiercest winds she could ever remember, arriving there as Mark came in for his noon meal.

She was not sure what explanation he had offered the manager and his wife for his removal from Wildfell. Probably none at all, but Mrs. Hawarth was cooking for him and she had evidently made the small morning room that faced onto the hills as comfortable as possible. A table was set before the window and there was a cheerful fire burning in the grate.

Mark rose as Janet came in.

"Hullo!" he said as Jonathan ran towards him, but his eyes were quite frankly questioning Janet's presence there.

"This came with the mail," she explained, holding out the cable. "I offered to bring it because old Mr. Soden had been this way before he delivered it at Wildfell."

Mark's expression sharpened, but when he had read the cable there was nothing but relief in his eyes.

"It's from Ruth," he said briefly. "She's on her way back from Canada."

Janet's immediate reaction was overwhelming joy, mingled with a certain amount of sadness as she thought of Harriet. If only Ruth had made her decision to return before her mother's death! Then, glancing at Mark, and seeing the relief on his face, she knew that there was something even more personal for her in Ruth's homecoming.

His sister's decision had solved Mark's most pressing problem. With Ruth at Wildfell—or the Grange—he would not need anyone else to look after Jonathan.

I can't be hurt anymore, Janet thought. *Not any more deeply than I have been already. When Ruth comes I must be ready to go.*

She was quite independent now. Miss Pope's legacy had been paid into her small bank account, and it would take care of the future. She could not look ahead to these empty days without pain, without feeling that the best of life had eluded her.

Mark was standing beside the window, the cable open on the table beside him, and suddenly she felt that there was something more to his sister's homecoming than just his relief at the thought of getting rid of her. She felt it so strongly that she was forced to ask, "Can I help in any way, Mark? I don't mean only about preparing a welcome for Ruth—I'll do that gladly   but if there's anything else I can do you have only to ask."

For a split second he hesitated and she caught her breath expectantly, ready to respond immediately if only she could ease some of the burden he had been carrying for so long. Then he said almost curtly, "There's no need to prepare a homecoming for Ruth. She may not come to the dale."

"But surely after all these years?" she protested. "I thought...."

He swung around, looking down searchingly into her face. His own was gray and strained, with deep shadows under the eyes.

"I've no idea how much you know of Ruth's story," he said harshly, "or how much Tom Ransome has seen fit to tell you, but Ruth will have another decision to make when she knows Ransome is back in Kirby Allerton." His mouth twisted with the old bitterness. "The dale may be too small to hold them both."

She could not answer that. Mark believed that she had Tom's fullest confidence, while all she knew was that Tom was still in love with Ruth. She knew it instinctively. It was something she had felt from the beginning, and she thought that Mark was being unnecessarily bitter about Tom's youthful marriage.

"Shall I tell Jonathan?" she asked. "It would be rather nice if he could look forward to meeting his only real aunt."

"Not just now." Mark's face looked grayer than ever as he turned from the window. "There's no need to unsettle him if things go wrong." He seemed to have forgotten the meal that had been set out for him, but presently he looked down at the array of dishes and said, "Will you and Jonathan have some of this? Mrs. Hawarth always provides twice as much as I can cope with in the middle of the day."

"But you're comfortable otherwise, Mark?" Janet asked awkwardly.

"Quite comfortable." He was helping Jonathan on to a chair and he did not look up. "My wants are really very few."

They sat down in silence.

"We'd like to thank you for the Christmas tree," Janet said at last.

"Please," Jonathan asked before Mark could reply, "can we have lights on it? 'Lectric lights, like Martha Crosby says they have on the village one in Allerton?"

Mark had done nothing further about wiring the rooms at Wildfell. Either he had not had the time or he had thought it unnecessary after his mother's death.

"I'll see what I can do," he promised, but he seemed to be looking beyond Jonathan, into the future.

"Will you go to Liverpool to meet Ruth?" Janet asked after Mark had passed the cable to her to read. "This says that the ship docks on the nineteenth."

"Yes," he said, pushing back his chair. "The day after tomorrow."

So soon! So soon! A small pulse beat wildly in Janet's throat, choking back any conventional utterance she might have tried to make. Christmas had seemed the major event on their horizon only a few hours ago, and now, even before Christmas, she might have left Wildfell.

"If you have packing to do," she offered, but Mark shook his head.

"Mrs. Hawarth will fling enough for a couple of nights into a bag for me. I can't afford to be away for long."

Janet felt dismissed, rising awkwardly to help Jonathan with the remainder of his pudding as Mrs. Hawarth came in to clear away. The farm manager's wife gave her a sharply inquisitive look, but even when Mark had gone she did not ask any questions. Janet supposed she might be resentful of her presence at the Grange, because Mark would be paying her well for her services and she would not want to lose a comparatively easy job.

"Who's coming from Canada?" Jonathan asked after a thoughtful pause when they were halfway up the dale road on their way back to Wildfell. "Is it someone called Ruth?"

"Yes." Mindful of Mark's warning, Janet did not want to pursue the conversation. We'll have to go to Kirby Allerton tomorrow and buy some decorations for the Christmas tree," she suggested instead. Despite Mark's earlier veto, she would have to take Jonathan now; he could not be left alone at Wildfell. "Musgrove's should have them. Or perhaps the post office."

"Can we go today?"

Janet glanced at her watch.

"No. Tomorrow, I think."

Jonathan looked up at the lowering heavens, screwing up his eyes and pursing his lips in the way Heber did when he was about to pass judgment on the weather.

"It'll snow tomorrow," he announced. "There's gray goose feathers in the sky."

Janet hugged him to her as they breasted the hill.

"You're a proper dalesman, Jonny!" she said with the faintest catch in her voice. "All right! We'll go to Kirby Allerton, if Heber can spare the time to take us in the car. We could never ride over the edge of the fell in this wind."

Heber, for once, did not put the usual obstacles in the way. He was not, apparently, averse to the trip, and Mark had put the old Morris at their disposal when he had bought the new car.

"Clickety-bang! Thump! Thump!" Jonathan sang out in time with the rickety old vehicle as they bumped along the narrow dale road. "Bang! Bang! Bang! We're going to Kirby Allerton for spangles for the tree!"

They tried Musgrove's and the post office to no avail.

"There's the new shop at the end of the main street, right at the very end." Jonathan was still hopeful, with only the edge of disappointment hovering in his voice. "You know. Beside Mr. Ransome's bungalow."

Janet had been thinking about Tom, but somehow she did not want to meet him at that moment with the news of Ruth's arrival so fresh in her mind.

"Do you think they will sell decorations?" she began doubtfully.

"They sell everything!" Jonathan was not to be put off without the most exhaustive search. " 'Sides, we can't go home without seeing Mr. Ransome's chickens."

That seemed to settle their destination so far as Jonathan was concerned, and in any case Tom was busy in his small paddock when they came out of the shop, triumphantly clutching a paper bag of decorations.

"We've got them! We've got them!" Jonathan shouted jubilantly. "We've got the spangly stuff for the tree, an' a star for the top, an' candles! Six different colors of candles," he added soberly as Tom lifted him over the gate.

"What excitement!" he grinned, peering into the bag. "That tree of yours is going to be worth looking at when it's finished."

"Yes," Jonathan nodded, "it will be." He walked around, looking into the chicken pens while Tom opened the gate for Janet.

"We mustn't stay," Janet told him. "Heber has brought us down in the old Morris."

"You've time for a cup of tea, surely?" They had caught up with Jonathan and Tom ruffled his hair. "You wouldn't say no to a fizzy lemonade, would you, Jonathan? Even in this weather?"

"No," said Jonathan, sliding a small hand into his. "I would like one very much." And then he added when they were not quite at the back door, "Ruth is coming from Canada."

The unexpectedness of it rushed the color into Janet's cheeks. She looked at Tom and caught her breath. His face was as white as a sheet.

"How long have you known?" he asked.

"The cable came this morning."

"For Mark, of course?"

"Yes."

He walked a little way along the gravel path and then came back to her side.

"Don't worry about this, Janet," he said thickly. "I know Mark's attitude upsets you, but   he's been justified, in a way. I deserve his contempt, if nothing more. I suppose he will go to meet Ruth?"

"Yes," Janet said. "She's docking at Liverpool tomorrow."

Jonathan came back to tug at her hand.

"Come on!" he urged. "Mrs. Bowes has got some tea ready."

Janet could hardly drink her tea. In spite of the effort he was making for Jonathan's benefit, she could see that Tom had received a severe shock. Ruth's coming had been too sudden for him. He had wanted more time to consider the future.

Yet, when he said goodbye to her half an hour later, his eyes were luminous.

"Don't think you've let Mark down by telling me this, Janet," he said. "In   a sort of a way I had a right to know."

On the way back to Wildfell Heber drove more quickly than usual.

"Sheep be still to bring down off t'Crag," he announced with a weather eye on the skyline above the distant Cleveland Hills. "Storm'll be a reet grand 'un when it cums."

ALL NEXT DAY there was an aura of expectancy about the dale. Even the high crags above the ridge seemed to be waiting, crouching more closely against the dead heather, their backs humped to the north. The sparse line of thorns fringing the moor stretched supplicant arms southward as if for protection, blown into grotesque shapes by the prevailing wind, but Wildfell stood four-square to it, contemptuous of its wrath.

Generations of sturdy hill farmers had lived out such storms in the shelter of these stout gray walls, and their flocks had survived in spite of loss. Janet felt a fierce, comforting pride as she looked from its windows up to the moor where the sheep were already sheltering, huddled in the lee of the gray stone dikes.

The first flakes of snow began to fall toward evening. Jonathan came shouting to the house place with them on his coat, watching with disappointment as they disintegrated before his eyes in the warmth.

"The snow won't last!" he mourned. "It won't lie!"

"It will outside," Janet consoled. The temperature was down to thirty degrees and the barometer was falling rapidly. She remembered winters when the road to Wildfell had been closed for days. "We'll have to build up the fire and get Heber to bring in more wood."

Heber came, shuffling his feet across the yard and stamping the snow from his boots on the house place floor. He had been down to the Grange and Janet wondered if he had brought any message from Mark.

"T'maister be gone to Liverpool," he said slowly. "It fair flays me how folks can gallivant t'cities when there's wark waitin' on t'moors. But Maister Hawarth's in charge at t'Grange, an' like as no' up here, an' all!" he grumbled. "Snow'll no' be ower deep while he's managin' everything!"

Janet built up the fire and put Jonathan to bed. The long evening stretched ahead of her and she tried to read, but thoughts of Mark and Ruth and Tom Ransome came between her and the printed page so often that she closed the book and let her head fall back against Harriet's chair.

In that familiar room, Harriet Langdon seemed very near, and Janet felt in need of some of Harriet's special brand of courage at that moment. Events seemed to be racing toward one inevitable end, and now she knew that Wildfell would hold her heart as securely as Mark did. This bleak, gray little farmhouse that huddled close against the fell was home. It was the only real home she had ever known. The years between did not count; their luxury and comparative idleness were almost a source of shame to her now, although in one way she did not regret them. They had brought her to a realization of what she really wanted in life.

Her eyes closed, and when she opened them again the world outside was very still. She crossed to the window, drawing aside the heavy velvet curtains she had hung there for Harriet's added comfort so short a while ago, but she could not see out. Thick snow had piled itself against the pane.

She made a hot drink for herself, carrying it up to her bedroom. The room itself was freezingly cold, the windows encrusted with ice even on the inside, and she shivered as she got between the sheets.

In the morning the snow was above the house place steps and Heber grunted and groaned outside as he attempted to clear a path for them. He was, in fact, working against odds, for the snow was falling as thickly as ever, drifting up against the outbuildings to the level of the barn windows in a spotless sheet of white.

Janet brought a shovel and began to dig. The soft, white snow was feather-light and as dry as cotton wool. She looked at Heber and then at the sky.

"There's more to come?" she asked.

"Ay, an' more after that," he answered dourly.

"Heber," she asked sharply, "do you think there's a risk of us being cut off?"

He straightened from his task, leaning his weight on the handle of the spade.

"It's happened afore," he said.

Janet cooked the breakfast and called Jonathan, who could scarcely eat for excitement. He wanted to be out in the snow, so she wrapped him up well after he had eaten his porridge and let him go with Heber. He was soon in again. The wind was vicious and his hands were cold.

Heber and the cowman were gathering the sheep down to the lower folds when Tom Ransome came up through the paddock.

He was covered in snow when Janet opened the door to him and for a split second she wondered if he needed help. The she saw his car standing at the gate, and realized that he had been unable to drive it into the yard because of the drifting snow. The road was still passable, but only just.

"Janet," he said, "I want you to come down to the village—you and the boy. There's plenty of room for you both at the bungalow."

She looked at him uncertainly as he shook the loose snow from his coat.

"You think it's going to get worse?"

"Much worse."

She hesitated.

"We're—prepared for it."

"Not on your own. Mark would never have left you here if he had thought this was on the way."

"It may not last."

He turned down the collar of his coat.

"I'm afraid I'm going to be adamant about this, Janet," he told her. "We're on the main road at Allerton and you're not. There's no reason why you should stay here and be marooned."

"There's Heber and the cowman."

"Heber will be only too pleased to get you out of his way. You will be a heavy responsibility to him otherwise."

"It's—terribly like deserting the ship."

"Don't talk nonsense!" he said briskly. "Your first loyalty is to Jonathan. There's nothing amusing about being snowed up in a house for days." He was beginning to look impatient. "Mark wouldn't thank you for taking such a risk when you can get away."

"Supposing the snow stops?"

"Then you can come back. No harm will be done. There's only the sheep to look after, and Heber and the cowman are quite capable of doing that. You couldn't help in any way."

She supposed Tom's argument was reasonable enough, and perhaps it was foolish to keep on thinking about holding the fort and that sort of thing. After all, her first loyalty *was* to Jonathan.

"If you'll wait," she said, "I'll get some things together and I'll have to explain to Heber."

"I'll do that," Tom said. "You get Jonathan ready."

The suggestion of urgency in his voice made her hurry. She was ready and waiting with Jonathan inside half an hour.

When they went out to the car Heber and the cowman were digging the accumulated snow away from the wheels. Heber seemed relieved that they were going.

"Ah can manage fine," he assured her. "Ah's best left to mysen."

Tom hurried her into the backseat, lifting Jonathan up in front.

"We'll just about make it," he said. "There's only one treacherous bit over the ridge and it hasn't started to freeze yet."

The journey was a nightmare. One skid would have put them in the ditch on that narrow, switchback road with its sudden bends and blind corners, and the snow drove straight into the windshield in madly dancing flakes that began to hold a paralyzing fascination in time.

Janet watched them with a swiftly beating heart. Supposing something did happen to the car? Supposing she had landed Jonathan in a far more precarious position than they would have been in if they had stayed at Wildfell?

Looking at Tom's broad back, she felt curiously reassured. He would not do anything foolish, and he had lived in the dale long enough to know all about road conditions and what they could safely attempt.

They drove across the ridge with the wind snarling at their heels, but almost immediately they began to drop down on the far side. It seemed to be hours, however, before they joined the main road and the first straggling houses came into sight. The little cottages stood like crouching gray ghosts on either side of the road, but they spelled safety and human habitation.

Janet drew a deep breath of relief.

"We're almost there," Tom said.

"Yes, I'm so glad." She looked down at Jonathan, wondering if the journey had tired him, but he seemed to be enjoying their adventure. "It was good of you to come, Tom," she added.

He looked ahead at the swirling white flakes.

"I think it was necessary," he said.

When they reached the bungalow Mrs. Bowes was waiting with a hot meal ready.

"In you go," Tom said. "I'll be with you just as soon as I've put the car away."

A sense of warmth and security enwrapped Janet

round as soon as she entered Tom's door. It embraced her, but it seemed to shelter Jonathan even more. She would never had left Wildfell if it had not been for the child, she realized, yet perhaps Mark would feel that Jonathan should have stayed there to become acclimatized to the rigors of the moor at an early age.

"He's only a child," Mrs. Bowes said, sitting Jonathan up in Tom's armchair to change his boots for a pair of warm slippers. "You'll both be far better here with Mr. Ransome." She gave Janet a quick, probing look. "He was fair worried about you up there on those moors when the snow started," she added. "He said he knew what Wildfell could be like if the dale was cut off and there was no way of getting through for days."

"He has lived out more than one siege at the Grange," Janet recalled with a smile. "And even that's a lot different from a small farm up on the open moor."

Mrs. Bowes got up from her knees, releasing Jonathan so that he could go to the window to watch for Tom.

"Mr. Ransome's heart is still over there on the other side o' Parson's Crag," she commented. "Pity he had to sell it all."

"It is a pity," Janet agreed. "But it's in good hands, Mrs. Bowes. Mr. Langdon won't neglect it."

"No, I suppose not." Some of the older woman's kindliness had suddenly been withdrawn. "Still, it's not the same, is it?" she wanted to know. "The Grange has been Ransome land for three hundred years, so I am told. It's quite a bit of time, when you come to think of it. All the family roots are there, and they served it and the dale well in their time."

"Perhaps Mr. Langdon will do just as well if he is given a chance," Janet pointed out in defense of Mark. "He's an excellent farmer."

"But not one to mix with his tenants much, is he?" Dora Bowes reflected. "The little lad is different, though!" She smiled as Jonathan rushed to open the back door for Tom. "Mr. Ransome thinks the world of him!"

There was nothing much Tom could do outside, so he built Jonathan a boat with some old wood he found in the kitchen and they sailed it joyfully in the bath for two hours while Janet helped Mrs. Bowes with her baking.

"Please let me do something," she had begged. "It will help to pass the time."

She knew that time would hang heavily for her till Mark got back. It seemed that the whole future stood suspended, waiting for his return. If he brought Ruth with him her own usefulness at Wildfell would be at an end, for somehow she knew that Ruth would stay in Comerdale if she did return.

Mark had been doubtful about Ruth, wondering, perhaps, if she would want to meet Tom again on the old familiar ground where each turn of the road must bring a poignant memory. Their youthful love had been something that the whole dale had known about, and Ruth might hesitate to renew the contact in case her heart might be torn asunder a second time.

Deep beneath the surface, however, Janet felt a strange current running, a swift, dark tide of hatred that she had seen reflected more than once in Mark Langdon's eyes. It had been masked by Mark's contempt, but the stronger emotion was there, held in check only by the thin barrier of an icy reserve.

Tom found her sitting darning Jonathan's socks before the living room fire.

"You make a pretty domesticated picture!" he smiled, settling down in the chair facing her and taking out his pipe. "The boat is in dry dock at the moment while

Jonathan helps Mrs. Bowes to grade the eggs. There aren't many, so he won't be long."

He filled his pipe and sat looking at her with it clasped loosely between his hands. Janet went on with her darning, her head bowed over the sock, the orange firelight picking out the auburn highlights in her smoothly brushed hair. She felt that Tom wanted to talk to her about something important but didn't know how or where to begin.

"Janet," he said, at last, "if you had made a—terrible mistake a long time ago and six years had passed without your being able to do anything about it, would you make an effort after all that time to rectify it? Even though you knew that the—other person must hate you pretty thoroughly for the anguish you caused them in the past?"

The sock fell from Janet's hands and she clasped them tightly above it.

"You mean Ruth?" she asked. "You're still in love with her, Tom?"

"I've never been in love with anyone else in my life," he said.

She did not ask why he had married someone else. He had said that he had made a mistake, and remembering Matthew Langdon's stern implacability, she knew the sort of opposition Ruth and he had been up against. When Ruth had taken the initiative and her courage in both hands and had fled to London, it had been too late.

That was as much as she knew of their story, and it had seemed far too little to foster a contemptuous hatred such as Mark's.

"Mark wants Ruth at Wildfell," she said slowly, "but I don't think he'll force the issue in any way. All along I've felt that he wants her to come back of her own free will—because she wants to come. Even when his mother was so ill, he didn't *send* for Ruth. I suppose he told her the facts and left it to her what she decided to do."

"That was my fault, too," he said heavily. "She didn't come back because of me."

Janet thought it unlikely. Mark, she felt sure, had not discussed Tom's return in his letters to Canada. But she fancied that that was one reason why he had gone to Liverpool to meet the boat.

Her heart began to beat slowly and heavily. So much would depend upon Ruth's reaction to that news, she thought. So much for them all.

Tom rose to his feet, thrusting the unlit pipe into his jacket pocket as Jonathan and Mrs. Bowes came into the room carrying plates and the tea tray. Janet felt that Tom's confidences might have gone further if there had not been this interruption, but during the remainder of the evening there was no opportunity to renew them. A neighboring farmer came to ask Tom's help with an ailing heifer, and Janet did not see her host again till morning.

Tom had not been to bed, but he emerged from the bathroom alert and newly shaven as she made her appearance at her bedroom door.

"That's the worst of a bungalow!" he said with a laugh. "You keep meeting people!"

Janet wondered if he often contrasted his present existence with the more spacious life he had lived at the Grange, but she did not think Tom was the type to brood unduly over his changed circumstances. His brown eyes were sometimes deeply shadowed, but it was the reflection of neither envy nor defeat.

"Jonathan has had his porridge," he announced. "The snow has stopped and he has gone out to dig his way across to the hen houses."

"I expect he's well enough wrapped up," Janet smiled. "He's not at all an indoor animal, is he?"

"Far from it. What's bred in the bone, I suppose, comes out in the flesh." There was frank envy in his voice. "I'd give anything for a lad like that, Janet," he added quietly.

Janet felt a strange contraction in her throat as she looked up at him. Surely Tom's life was not going to be spoiled by the frustration of loving where it was not returned? Six years could have changed Ruth, but she prayed that they had not.

"There must be some happiness for you, Tom, somewhere," she said unsteadily. "You seem to deserve it."

He looked down at her with a smile in his eyes, but doubt was there, too.

"Do we ever really *deserve* happiness unless we make it for others?" he asked. "We're hotheaded and harebrained and unthinking, and we pile all sorts of misery on other people's doorsteps without a qualm, apparently. We think of ourselves so often that it's what hurts *us* that matters more than not. It's all very selfish, you see, but we don't look at it that way till it's too late, perhaps. Some of us never see it."

"Perhaps it isn't too late for you, Tom," Janet said. "Somehow I feel that Ruth will come back."

He followed her into the living room without answering. Mrs. Bowes had built up a huge fire and it roared fiercely up the chimney in defiance of the outside cold; for Janet spread out her hands toward it, as if she had sudden, urgent need of its comforting warmth.

"It hasn't been such a violent storm as we imagined it would be," she said, looking out through the window to the white road and the snow-laden branches of the trees on its far side. "Perhaps we should have stayed at Wildfell, after all."

"It may not be over yet," Tom warned, coming to stand behind her while he waited for the coffee to percolate into the pot. "The sky is still pretty heavy with it over there in the north, and the wind's still like ice."

Janet was thinking that she should never have left the farm. If Mark came back and wanted to see her, he would have all this extra way to come. She felt restless and uneasy as Tom went to bring more wood for the fire.

"Keep your eye on the percolator," he warned. "It's a pressure affair and liable to blow up at any moment! Mrs. Bowes is scared stiff of the thing, but it's really quite easy to manage."

Janet stood over the sizzling contraption, watching the dark liquid being forced in a steady stream into the pot, her thoughts a good many miles away in Comerdale, so that the first ring at the front doorbell went almost unnoticed by her.

Automatically she had expected Tom to answer it, but when it came again, more loudly and more insistently, it seemed, she realized that Tom must still be in the woodshed across the yard and Mrs. Bowes out of earshot as she cut a path with Jonathan toward the hen coops. She went out into the narrow hall and opened the front door.

Almost without surprise she recognized the man standing there with snow on his boots and a look of icy control in his gray eyes.

"Mark!"

"I've come for Jonathan," he said without preliminaries. It was almost as if he would have swept her aside, out of his path. "Is he here?"

"Yes." Her voice was so faint that she wondered if he would hear her explanation at all. "We thought we were going to be snowed in at Wildfell, and Tom brought us down here to be on the main road in case the dale was cut off."

Mark did not speak. His eyes held a blazing fury that scorched her without the accompaniment of words.

"I suppose you disagree?" she asked unsteadily. "But the gale was dreadful yesterday—all day. Even Heber thought that we should go."

Mark looked down at her coldly.

"I haven't come for an explanation of why you are here, Janet," he said. "I have come for Jonathan. You have every right to please yourself where or whom you come to in an emergency. I got through to Wildfell early this morning and found you missing. Heber told me where you were." His mouth was grim and hard, his voice harsh with the force of his anger, which he seemed barely able to control. "Whatever you intend to do is your own affair, but Jonathan's whereabouts is mine. Will you get him ready, please? I'm taking him back to the Grange."

Janet felt frozen to the spot. Mark's contemptuous anger cut her like a knife, so that she could no longer argue with him. Her explanation had been brushed aside as immaterial to the situation. All he wanted was the child.

She turned, aware of Tom in the background, standing just inside the open kitchen door. He was carrying a big, brassbound tub of logs and he set it down as she went toward him, but he did not seem to see her.

"Tom!" she said, as if to ward off a blow, but he did not hear.

Pale and tense, he stood quite still, staring at Mark silhouetted in the open doorway against the snow.

"You're here for Jonathan?" he asked in a deep, restrained voice that did not seem to be his. "Will you come in?"

"No," Mark said, "I'll wait here. I've asked Janet to bring him."

Janet did not move. The look on Tom's pale, drawn face kept her where she was. Tom made a movement toward the outer door, and she saw the sudden determination in his eyes that made them almost as ruthless as Mark's.

"There's something I have to ask you, Mark," he said steadily. "Is Jonathan your son?"

Mark did not flinch. It almost seemed as if he had expected Tom's question, as if he had been waiting for it and had his answer ready.

"No," he admitted bitterly. "But neither is he yours. You have no claim to him. You have forfeited any right you could have had. He belongs to Ruth."

In the stillness Janet heard Tom draw a long, shuddering breath.

"I see," he said and turned away. He looked stunned and defeated, his shoulders hunched forward as if the load they bore was too much for them now that he felt its full and crushing weight for the first time. "I'll ask my housekeeper to bring him."

Janet was left facing Mark across the narrow hall, her lips too stiff to move, even in protest.

"I'm sorry if this has been a shock to you," he said coldly. "It may ease the situation between you and Ransome, however, if I confirm the fact that he could not have known about Jonathan before this."

"Mark," she breathed, "that doesn't count! What I think doesn't come into this. Not just now. It's—Ruth that matters. Ruth and Tom."

He looked at her as if he was not quite sure of what she had said, and then Jonathan came running through the kitchen door, bringing a flurry of snow with him and an icy blast of cold air that seemed to penetrate straight down into Janet's heart.

"Why aren't you coming with us?" he asked when he heard that he was going back to Comerdale with Mark. "Why aren't you coming to Wildfell, Janet?"

"We are going to the Grange," Mark said, picking him up before Janet could answer. "Wildfell may still be cut off if it snows again."

Was that Mark's way of telling her that this might be their final parting? Feeling stricken and rejected, Janet turned slowly back into the living room, waving from the window to Jonathan without really seeing him. Hot, scalding tears ran down her cheeks, blurring her vision, and her heart beat slowly and heavily as she listened to the car drawing away. They were all caught up in this hopeless web of the past and she might never see Mark or Wildfell again.

A firm hand on her shoulder made her aware of Tom. It was heavy with kindly sympathy as he guided her toward the hearth.

"What a mess I've made of everything, Janet," he said. "And now I've involved you without really meaning to."

She sat down in the chair he pulled forward, automatically accepting the cup of coffee he poured for her.

"Drink it," he said. "It may help to warm you."

She felt completely frozen, but she managed to look across the hearth at him with all her sympathy for him welling in her eyes.

"Of course, Mark's bitter," he said. "It's not exactly a story to be proud of, but when I 'married' Ruth I had no idea that my wife was alive."

Janet sat tensed in her chair, staring at him incredulously.

"Didn't you know?" Tom asked. "Didn't Mark tell you?"

"Mark never made a confidante of me." Janet had to moisten her lips before she could go on. "I suppose he had never been able to trust me since I let him down all those years ago."

"You were only a kid," Tom said defensively. "It was easy enough for you to make a mistake in the circumstances. We all want to try our wings at one time or another. Mark should have known that you regretted it when you agreed to come back to Wildfell."

"Mark didn't want me to come," she said unsteadily. "I asked to come. I wrote to his parents and I thought that Matthew Langdon cabled me to come, but it was Mark. I didn't know his father was dead."

"If the old devil had been dead six years ago," Tom said bitterly, "all this wouldn't have happened. He stood between Ruth and me with a fiendish determination to separate us for some damnably selfish reason of his own, and when I couldn't persuade Ruth to come away with me then and there and defy him, I rushed off to London like a fool and married someone else." He got up and began to pace the small room. "Heavens, Janet! What utter idiots we can be when we imagine that life has cheated us or that it's hopeless to look for the full measure of happiness or even to wait too long for it! We rush off and do some mad, impulsive thing that we regret forever afterward. I married a cheap little actress. I met her two days after I arrived in London, where I had gone because I thought the dale wouldn't hold Ruth and me any longer. I must have broken my father's heart when I went away, but maybe I didn't care about that sort of thing, either. I was full of self-pity and a determination to grasp whatever life had left to offer me. I married the sort of person I deserved, I suppose, and Lucia didn't hesitate. I was talking wildly about going anywhere in the world so long as I didn't return to Comerdale, and somehow she knew that I had the money to indulge that sort of whim."

He pulled up before the window, looking out at the snowbound landscape as if he could see the dark procession of the past filing slowly across its unmarked purity.

"Don't go on, Tom, if it hurts too much," Janet advised him. "I didn't know about all this. The only thing I knew was that you had gone to London and married, and that Ruth had left the dale. Mark never mentioned you except—to let me see in no uncertain way that he would not have you at Wildfell."

"Can you blame him, after the mess I've made of his sister's life?" Tom asked bitterly.

"No." She had to be truthful. "I don't suppose we can, Tom. Mark seemed to have no forgiveness in him."

He look around sharply.

"He hasn't forgiven you?"

She shook her head.

"He was madly—wildly in love with you, Janet," Tom said.

"That was long ago." She clasped her hands together in her lap, her fingers pressed tightly, willing herself not to let the tears gather in her eyes again. "I failed Mark. I turned down his love."

"But you came back!" Tom protested. "That should have let him see you still cared about him." He turned from the window and stood looking down at her bowed head. "Anyway, why did he send for you? Why did he let you come?"

"To look after his mother and Jonathan." She looked up with the faintest hint of a smile. "Mark's hard, Tom. He didn't make it easy for me when I first came back to the dale. He didn't intend to spare me the tasks I had rejected and scorned six years ago, but that was nothing. I think I wanted to do them to show him how sorry I was, in a way. He was as hard as flint in that respect, but he would have died a thousand deaths to spare his mother one added touch of sorrow."

Tom flinched.

"I realize that," he said contritely. "I—don't suppose he ever let her know about—Ruth and me."

"No." Janet was utterly sure about that. "Mark took the responsibility for Jonathan to spare his mother the truth. Not to spare Ruth. He wanted the boy brought up at Wildfell," she added unsteadily, "and if there were other things he wanted—more land and more power and more money—they were primarily for—your son."

Tom buried his face in his hands and sank into a chair.

"My God, Janet, what am I going to do?" he cried. "Ruth and I had five days together. Five wonderful, unforgettable days in which we believed ourselves man and wife. We had married quietly in London three months after I had been told that my wife had been killed in an accident in Malaya. She had gone out to Singapore with some dancing troupe or other after she refused to give up her career and come home with me to the Grange. I could only think of her death as a happy release for me at the time, but I had no right to persuade Ruth into another hasty marriage. She wanted to wait. She wanted to come home to the dale, but I convinced her we could do that afterward. Now I realize that we were both still half-afraid of her father. He had a strange power over Ruth, which he had exerted since her earliest childhood." He drew in a deep quivering breath. "But you know all that, Janet. Matthew Langdon made your own life pretty miserable in his time."

"He was always harsh and exacting," Janet admitted, "but he gave me a roof over my head, and I should have been grateful for that fact alone."

"The man had a mania for power," Tom said bitterly.

"He thought that he possessed his family, body and soul, and that made Ruth hopelessly afraid of him. My poor Ruth! She must have suffered agonies when she knew about the child!" He struck his clenched fist against his brow, as if to hammer his tortured thoughts into some kind of order. "It all happened with the swiftness of a nightmare. We had our stolen honeymoon, and when I got back to London there was a message waiting for me to say that my wife's death had not been proved, after all. It had all been a ghastly mistake. The unknown woman thought to be Lucia had been identified as someone else three months later."

He got up and paced to the window again, looking out at the snow.

"We did the only thing we could possibly do in the circumstances," he ended in a flat, dead voice. "Ruth and I parted. I thought that was all there was to it. Unutterable happiness, briefly realized. But now it seems there was a child. Jonathan!"

He stood staring before him, his world collapsed around him.

"It's fantastic," he said after a bit. "Almost impossible to believe, isn't it? Ruth's back in the dale—at the Grange—and I'm here on the other side of the fell." Suddenly he straightened, as if the words had unlocked some door in his mind. "If she *has* come back, I'm free to go to her! Free beyond any doubting, at last!" He swung around to face Janet with insistent demand in his eyes for the first time. "Do you think she knew that I was here?" he asked.

"Yes," Janet said, quite sure that Mark would have told Ruth.

"Then, if she had come back—if she *has*—she's come knowing that we would meet!" He looked about him like a man who has found food for hope at the eleventh hour. "I'm going to the Grange, Janet," he said. "I've got to find out why she has come home."

Janet went with him to the door, watching as he got his shabby old car out of the garage and drove away in the direction of Comerdale. He went the long way around, to the south end of the dale, and he would be lucky if he reached Scarton Grange before the snow began to fall again.

Janet did not know what he would find there. Ruth—or a Mark so enraged by his coming that their meeting might very well end in blows. She wondered if she should have kept Tom at the bungalow until she was sure of Ruth's presence at the Grange. Mark had not said that Ruth had come back with him. All he had said was that Jonathan belonged to Ruth.

But he belonged to Tom, too. Janet felt that she could not sit still, yet she could not leave the bungalow, either, in case Tom should return and have need of her.

THE HOURS OF WAITING seemed endless. Mrs. Bowes prepared a noon meal for three, but still Tom did not return. Janet's heart began to beat heavily at the thought of all that might have happened since Tom had left them, of tempers roused, perhaps, and injury inflicted.

If there had been any way of following Tom to Scarton Grange she thought that she would have taken it and braved Mark's increasing wrath rather than go on sitting through this endless time of waiting.

The snow held off, but the sky was so heavily laden with it that it was dark by three o'clock.

"I'll slip down to the shops before it gets too dark," Mrs. Bowes suggested, putting her head round the sitting-room door for the third time since they had cleared away the untouched meal, to see if her guest was still all right. "I won't be long."

Janet rose to draw the curtains, but she hesitated to shut out the last of the light. The fire was bright, casting flickering shadows on the ceiling. Bright enough for her to sit and wait by. It was like a hundred evenings long ago when they had sat at Wildfell waiting for the men to come in off the hill. Mark and his father coming into the houseplace, wet through after their daylong struggle with the sheep but satisfied with the result of their labors and content to settle by the fire with a hot meal set before them and only the dogs to put out at the ending of the day.

A primitive existence some might call it, but Janet knew that it was full and rewarding to men like Mark Langdon and Tom Ransome, whose roots were deep and firmly embedded in their native soil.

A sound outside made her turn from the fire, but she supposed it to be Mrs. Bowes coming back from the village and did not get up. When the bell rang through the silent hall she started to her feet almost in alarm.

The front door was closed and bolted. She opened it with trembling fingers, seeing the figure in the half-light without recognizing Ruth for a moment.

"Janet!" Ruth said. "After all this time!"

Janet felt herself folded in two strong young arms with all the years between slipping away. Eagerly, jealously almost, she pulled Ruth in out of the cold.

"I'm so glad!" she cried. "I'm so glad you've come!"

Their friendship had always been a warm, generous thing, and now it seemed stronger than ever. Janet felt herself clinging to it as if Ruth, who had always come to her for courage and wisdom in the past, was now the one who had most to give.

"Take off your coat," she said. "I'll make some tea.

Tom's housekeeper has gone to the village, but she'll soon be back with the bread."

She went to fill the kettle, and when she came back Ruth was standing in the center of the room, looking around her with a gentle light in her eyes.

"It isn't difficult to imagine Tom being happy here," she mused softly. "It was the sort of life we planned."

Janet crossed to her side, unable to doubt the deep note of fulfillment in Ruth's voice.

"You were at the Grange when he got there?" she asked.

Ruth nodded.

"Yes. I think I knew he would come." There was a shining happiness in her gray eyes now that transcended all former sorrow and blotted out the past. "We are going to be married, Janet, just as soon as it can be arranged."

Janet's eyes were full of tears.

"You've waited so long, Ruth," she said. "And so patiently."

Ruth crossed to the fire, the glow from the burning logs throwing her strong features into sharp relief.

"I didn't know I was waiting," she said in a low, controlled voice. "There didn't seem to be any hope that Tom would be free one day to marry me. Our whole world had collapsed about us that day when we returned from France to find the message from Singapore waiting for Tom." Her eyes were suddenly dark with the pain of memory. "Why, oh, why did they take *three whole months* to find out the truth about Lucia's death!" Her clasped hands twisted nervously as she returned for a moment to the sharpest agony of the past. "I was bewildered and Tom was in utter despair, but we knew that he had to go back to Lucia. He had to find her. She was somewhere out there in Malaya and she might have needed him." Ruth drew in a deep breath that was almost a sigh. "It was Mark who saved me from complete collapse in those days, Janet. He had come to London and he found me soon after Tom and I had parted. He urged me to come back to the dale—to come home. He offered to bring me back, but when I discovered I was to have Tom's child I couldn't face it. I was an absolute coward. I was terrified of my father, and Mark knew that it would have killed mother in her weak state of health."

Ruth held out her hands to the fire, looking at the square fingers etched against its amber glow.

"My father's harshness cowed me in my youth, Janet," she went on. "I was never really brave enough to face up to him—not even to his displeasure—and his anger terrified me. The thought of it blunted my sense of right and wrong. Mark looked after me in London till Jonathan was born, and then, because he knew how weak and cowardly I really was, he offered to take Jon. He offered to accept full responsibility for his future so that I could start afresh. I chose Canada because it seemed far enough away to mean a new beginning, but now I know that you can't leave your conscience behind you, no matter how far you run. I realized that almost as soon as I got there, but I couldn't come back because of my mother and because of all Mark had accepted in my name."

She turned to the window, looking out into the quiet night. "Is there any wonder that Mark has been bitter!" she said. "We've all let him down, Janet, in our separate ways. He never thought I would give up my child and run away, and he must have felt the utmost contempt for me when I did it, although he said nothing. He kept his part of the bargain till the last. My mother never knew." She came back to the hearth. "There's just one thing, Janet. I was on my way home—or nearly so—when I got the cable telling me about her death. I wanted my child, scandal or

no scandal. Was that weakness, too? Was it selfishness on
my part, after all Mark had done?"

"It was—a natural thing to do," Janet said unsteadily.

"You've got to understand Mark's bitterness," Ruth
went on after a pause. "He felt that we had both been let
down by love. It hardened him, and so I don't suppose he
cared very much what was thought about him when he
brought Jonathan back to the dale. He kept the truth
from mother to shield me and to spare her, but he would
not try to explain himself to anyone else. Yet, I know that
he wanted me to come back—*because I wanted my son.* I
don't think Mark could ever understand my putting the
breadth of the Atlantic between me and my child."

Janet was seeing Mark now as he really was, but it did
not follow that he loved her still and could forgive her.

"Tom brought me down here in his car," Ruth said,
"but I would like to get back as quickly as possible." She
accepted her cup of tea from Janet with a tender smile
playing at the corners of her mouth. "It will soon be
Jonathan's bedtime."

Janet felt her heart contract with a pain that was
almost physical.

"Mark let him run riot just at first," she tried to say
evenly, "but I managed to convince him that a set bedtime
was absolutely necessary."

She seemed to be talking through a haze of pain,
unaware of how sharply Ruth was observing her.

"Won't you come back to the Grange with us?" Ruth
asked when she rose to put her cup down on the table.
"Tom will have to drive me back."

"I couldn't," Janet said in a stifled whisper. "Mark has
you to look after Jonathan now. There's no need for me
to come."

Ruth did not answer. She went to the front door and

stood waiting for Tom, who had picked up Mrs. Bowes and some extra groceries in the village. Ruth wanted them to take back with her to the Grange, and Tom did not seem greatly surprised when she said they would be going alone.

"You're welcome to stay here, Janet," he said, "as long as you like. I'm going to London tomorrow morning to fix up a few things, and it will be easier for me to go straight from the Grange."

So Mark had accepted him? Their differences were at an end, and it only remained for Ruth and Tom to be married quietly in London for everything to be right again, for three lives to run smoothly and peace to reign between Scarton and Wildfell, at last.

Mark's first disillusionment had been smoothed away, but Janet felt that he would never forgive her for her own unfaithfulness. His anger and humiliation and disappointment with Ruth and Tom were over now, but that did not affect her in any way. All it meant was that her period of usefulness at Wildfell was definitely at an end.

CHAPTER SEVEN

THE SNOW HELD OFF all that night and far into the next day. Janet looked at the sky and assured herself that the worst of the blizzard was over and she could safely return to Wildfell for her clothes. She could not embarrass Mark by remaining there when Ruth and Tom returned to Scarton Grange as man and wife.

There was absolutely no doubt in her mind that Mark would go back to Wildfell to live there alone, although he might still keep a controlling hand on most of the Scarton land. Wildfell was the remote aerie he would choose for himself, with only Heber and the cowman to work the hill with him.

Would he, she wondered, be content with that?

There did not seem any doubt about it, and she set out for the farm on the moor with a heart as heavy as lead.

The way was difficult on foot and impossible by any other means. The deep, soft snow gave at every other step, and she was exhausted long before she reached the crest of the hill and saw the ridge running across the open moor like a white mountain range. It was scarred and black at the edges where it fell sheer to the moor, and it seemed to cut her off completely from the more gentle reaches of the hidden dale on its far side, sealing her into a wild and desolate world where no hope or no kindness remained.

The road to Wildfell stretched before her, a narrow, twisting track, untrodden save for the mark of sheep at its edges and the imprint of a bird's claw where it had rested on its lone flight across the treeless waste.

She shivered, biting her teeth into her lower lip to keep it steady and heading determinedly south in the direction of the farm.

Soon the gray ridge of the roof came into sight and she saw Wildfell under its canopy of snow. It seemed to spring from the moor itself, part of it, gouging its strength from the gray rock that was so near the surface that nothing would survive there but the rough grass that was only suitable for sheep. She saw it in all the primitive starkness of its utter isolation, but she still loved it.

Heber and the cowman were busy in the folds, spreading straw and attending to the weaker ewes that had been brought down from the hill, and they looked up in surprise when they saw her.

Heber informed her that Mark had just gone, and Janet's heart gave a quick leap of mingled disappointment and relief. Perhaps it had been foolish of her to come, but she had not expected Mark to return so soon. She imagined him at the Grange, staying there at least till Tom and Ruth returned.

Nervously she climbed the narrow oak staircase to her room, pulling out drawer after drawer to pack her few belongings in a dumb agony of grief. This was the end, the last of happiness. She and Mark had come to the final parting of their ways.

She snapped the locks of her suitcase closed and stumbled with it down the stairs. It was darker than she would have expected for that time of day, and even before she reached the back door she knew that the snow was falling again. It came down in great flakes as big as coins, lying soft and white on the trampled yard, as if to cover up the footprints a man had made there earlier in the morning on his return to his home.

Janet stood staring out at the beginning of the storm until the whole yard was covered, and then she left her bag just inside the door where Mark would see it on his return, and went out into the softly falling snow. She would ask him to send the bag on to her at Kirby Allerton.

It was not dark and she knew the way. Every foot of the way, she tried to assure herself as she stumbled up the narrow road. Five miles to Kirby Allerton and the security of Tom's bungalow. Five miles by the dale road, but only two by the path that went under Parson's Crag.

The snow slanted toward her, each hurrying flake seeming to converge on her body in a fascinating swirl of white, and when they started to come more thickly they seemed to obscure her vision altogether. She took the path to the crag. *It's shorter*, she thought, *and perhaps the storm won't last.*

Up and up, stumbling and sliding on the rutted, dangerous track until she began to wish that she had kept to the road, after all. She was daleswoman enough to know that she dared not miss the path, and she realized that she would have been safer on the more frequented road where she would have had the snow posts to guide her, marking the way she had to go.

She could not turn back now, however. Not when she had almost gained the crag.

Remembering how difficult the path was at the top, she tried not to think of its dangers. The snow had thickened, and it swirled fiercely against her as she climbed higher, and almost forcing her back, but she was too near her objective now to give up.

As she approached the crag itself there was another banshee wailing, which set her nerves on edge and chilled her to the bone.

For a moment she could not move. She stood with her back against the cold, gray bulk of the crag and closed her eyes. A terrible weakness possessed her and she felt her legs giving way, but she struggled up again, clinging to the rock.

It was almost dark now, with visibility cut down to inches, and the conditions seemed worse on this north-western side of the ridge. She could not see at all. The snow rushed into her face, blinding her, and when she tried to go on the path was lost.

She knew where it should be, but the ground before her seemed to slope away into a merciless white oblivion, and for the first time she knew fear. It caught her by the throat like a strangling hand, and even when she tried to shake it off the thought of it was there at the back of her mind.

Once she slipped, hurtling down an icy slope to find herself at the foot of it, immersed in a deep white trough of snow that choked and blinded her for a moment before she climbed out, shaken and bewildered, to search for the path again.

She could not find it. It lay hidden beneath the first snowfall of the day before and there had not been any traffic that way to clear it. She knew then, beyond doubting, that she had been a fool to come that way.

She had come to get away from Mark! The thought struck her as ludicrous, but she had not wanted to embarrass him when he returned to Wildfell. What a fool she had been to think that he would ever have cared about her being there, that it would have mattered to him! He would have found some way of relieving himself of her presence, coolly and deliberately, at the first possible opportunity.

A sob choked in her throat, but she forced it back. This was no time for self-pity or even for regret. She had to get back to the shelter of the crag as best she could. It was the only way. The rocks up there were high and there were loose boulders on the ridge, on the more sheltered southerly side.

Almost on her hands and knees she made the difficult

ascent, stumbling into ruts and sinking knee-deep into unexpected drifts that looked firm and innocent enough when she first came to them.

Long afterward, she wondered how she had ever made the effort to regain the crag. The cold had pierced right through her, leaving her numb and shaken, and the wind tore at her malignantly, buffeting her as she struggled on, but the crag loomed ahead at last. It materialized so suddenly that she drew back subconsciously from its towering bulk, and then she was sinking down thankfully in the comparative shelter of its lee side, breathless and shivering from head to foot.

Now that she was out of the wind she did not seem to care so much. She crouched against the rock, doubling her legs under her for added warmth, and closed her eyes. The terrible banshee wailing that came down between the rocks was muted a little and she was no longer deafened by it. Gradually, very gradually, the ice in her limbs began to melt before a strange, burning heat. She no longer thought of escape. She was content to stay there.

The wind filled all her mind, but it had grown distant, like the wailing between the rocks, and a peculiar numbing peace took possession of her fears. She watched the snow covering her footprints, blotting them out as if they had never been.

Hours afterward, it seemed, there was another sound, a deep, insistent calling that stirred life in her, but she could not respond. She thought, foolishly, that it was Mark's voice, and found herself smiling faintly at the idea.

"Janet! Jan, are you there?"

Mark would not come for her. He would not know where she was, and perhaps he would not care. . . .

"Janet! Janet, answer me!"

The command was unmistakable. She tried to struggle to

her feet, but there was a crippling weakness in her limbs and she could not move.

"Here!" she called in a shadow of a voice. "Here, Mark—"

Quivering, she was aware of Mark standing above her, strong and square against the gray light, looking down at her with an expression in his eyes that she had never thought to see there again. He bent without a word and lifted her, holding her pressed closely against him.

"You're all right," he said harshly. "You're going to be all right now."

He held her till the quivering ceased, pressing her head down against his shoulder so that she could no longer see the snow nor feel the chilling cold of the searching wind, and she clung to him like a child, not caring that he could see and guess her need of him.

"How did you find me?" she asked unsteadily, and thought that he smiled a little grimly before he replied.

"By instinct, I think. Nobody else would have expected you to get away from Wildfell by this method."

She still clung to him, unable to let him go.

"I didn't want to get away, but I had to, Mark, when I knew you were coming back."

The confession had come quite simply, as if nothing but the truth would suffice between them now. Mark held her from him, looking down searchingly into her eyes.

"Didn't you know we could never escape each other?" he demanded. "It would have been—like this in the end, no matter how hard we had struggled." His arms tightened about her and his eyes lighted suddenly with a fiercely possessive light. "You were mine from the beginning, Jan, and though I suffered agonies of jealousy over your friend Grantley, and even over Tom Ransome, I think I must have realized that. I brought you back to Wildfell so that I could denounce my own love, so that I could force myself to reject you even when I saw you day by day, but it didn't work. I meant to live with you in the same house and forget that we had ever been in love, and I suppose that I meant to punish you, too. I meant to hurt you if I could." He drew in a swift breath. "Not a very noble reason for bringing you back, was it? Not the sort of reason that a lover might choose."

"There was your mother, too," Janet reminded him gently. "And Jonathan."

"Don't make excuses for me, Jan," he said unevenly. "My bitterness was so great at one time that it could have spoiled our love." His hands tightened over her arms as his eyes searched hers for the answer he needed. "Has it?" he demanded. "Has it?"

"Nothing could do that," Janet whispered. "Nothing ever, Mark!"

Instantly his lips came down on hers, kissing her silently, possessively, gently.

"So many reasons!" he said. "But deep down there must have been only one, Jan. I wanted you. Above all else, I loved you."

Half carrying her, half leading her, he made his way back into the dale with the assurance that had always been typical of him. He did not ask her if she could weather the difficult journey. He took it for granted that they would make it together, and if there was any anxiety in him when she stumbled on the way, he hid it from her till they reached the farm.

Janet didn't know whether it would have been easier to take the shorter way or not. They could have gone on down the other side of the ledge to Kirby Allerton, but Mark had not considered it. There was only one way, and that was back to the dale.

When they reached Wildfell, Heber had a huge fire

burning in the house place and Mark had unpacked her
case and set out her dressing gown and slippers for just
such an emergency. The slippers lay on the hearth in
Harriet's sitting room, and her heart gave a strange little
bound of joy at sight of them. Mark had known she
would come back! He had set out in search of her determined to bring her back to Wildfell.

How like him that was! How sure he was once he had
taken a situation in hand!

Looking at him in the leaping firelight, however, she
was not so certain of that assurance all of a sudden. There
seemed to be a new hesitancy about him that made her
smile very tenderly as she held out her arms to him.

"Mark," she whispered, "I've come home!"

Smothered in his passionate embrace, she looked over
his shoulder at the still shabby room, her eyes shining, her
heart beating strongly against his own.

"We'll find something better than this," he promised,
kissing her throat. "I'll build farther down the dale,
nearer Scarton, where it won't be so rough."

She silenced his pledge with her fingers against his lips.

"Don't change it, Mark," she begged. "We loved each
other here. I want it always to be like this!"

He laughed and kissed her agin, and the sound of his
laughter ran into her heart like sunlight across a darkened
stream.

"We'll build onto it in time," he promised. "We'll make
changes, but we'll make them together."

"Yes," she said. "Always together from now on!"

They stood in the firelight, looking out on the falling
snow, and it seemed to make a barrier between them a
the rest of the world. It was a barrier Janet did not want
sweep away. They were here together, on the same side o
it, here at Wildfell, where they belonged.